Blaze™

Dear Reader,

This is a sappy, sentimental love letter to all of you who've welcomed me back to the Harlequin Blaze line and taken the Sons of Chance miniseries into your homes and your hearts. Thank you for all the funny and appreciative emails and for your continued support of my books, whether you're reading them in paperback or on your ereader. You rock!

Because you've embraced the Sons of Chance with such enthusiasm, I'm going to keep writing books about them! So get ready for another summer of gorgeous cowboys coming at you in 2013. I have you and my wonderful editor, Brenda Chin, to thank for it, and I'm thrilled! Life at the Last Chance Ranch has become part of me, and I didn't want to say goodbye to all those folks I've come to love.

But I'm getting ahead of myself. We're still in the summer of 2012, and you're holding book nine in your hands. While I hope you've read all the others, you might have missed some. I realize that and I try really hard to make each book stand alone. So whether you're a frequent visitor to the Last Chance Ranch or a newcomer, I have a feeling that Rafe and Meg, best man and maid of honor at a traditional ranch wedding, will touch your heart and make you smile.

Be sure and pay attention to the epilogue, though, because it'll give you a hint about book ten!

Continuing to be yours,

Vicki Lewis Thompson

Vicki Lewis Thompson

FEELS LIKE HOME

HARLEQUIN®
entertain, enrich, inspire™

Recycling programs
for this product may
not exist in your area.

ISBN-13: 978-0-373-79703-5

FEELS LIKE HOME

ABOUT THE AUTHOR

New York Times bestselling author Vicki Lewis Thompson's love affair with cowboys started with the Lone Ranger, continued through Maverick and took a turn south of the border with Zorro. She views cowboys as the Western version of knights in shining armor—rugged men who value honor, honesty and hard work. Fortunately for her, she lives in the Arizona desert, where broad-shouldered, lean-hipped cowboys abound. Blessed with such an abundance of inspiration, she only hopes that she can do them justice. Visit her website at www.vickilewisthompson.com.

Books by Vicki Lewis Thompson

HARLEQUIN BLAZE

*Sons of Chance

To get the inside scoop on Harlequin Blaze and its talented writers, be sure to check out blazeauthors.com.

All backlist available in ebook. Don't miss any of our special offers. Write to us at the following address for information on our newest releases.

Harlequin Reader Service
U.S.: 3010 Walden Ave., P.O. Box 1325, Buffalo, NY 14269
Canadian: P.O. Box 609, Fort Erie, Ont. L2A 5X3

With thanks to Tony Horvath for creating
such fabulous covers for the Sons of Chance.
I'm blessed!

Prologue

August 23, 1980
from the diary of Eleanor Chance

I THINK MOST FOLKS IN Shoshone, Wyoming, would say that I'm a nonviolent sort. In fact, ask anyone in the entire Jackson Hole area who knows me, and they'll tell you I'm a calm woman not prone to outbursts of rage.

So these same people might be shocked to learn that I could, given the opportunity, twist Diana Chance's head right off her scrawny neck. I've never been so fired up in my entire life, which includes the time that my dear husband, Archie, forgot my birthday AND our anniversary in the space of a month.

If I had Diana in my clutches, nothing would save her except a promise to stay and be a devoted mother to my sweet little grandson, Jack, and a wife to my son, Jonathan. But the irresponsible piece of baggage has LEFT. She's abandoned both my son and my grandson, and for that I will never forgive her.

I hated the fighting between Jonathan and Diana, but I hate this more. No child should have to grow up knowing that his mother didn't love him enough to stick around. I will do all in my power to make it up to this poor little boy, but he's not even two. How can he be expected to understand?

All he knows is that his mother is gone. Her note tells us not to try and find her. Believe me, I've considered it. I have a little money put away, and I could hire a P.I. to track her down, but then what? Other than twisting her head from her neck, what do I want with her?

I want what I can't have, which is for her to be a good mother to my grandson and a good wife to my son. It's not possible. Archie tells me to let it go, that dwelling on it is useless and will make me even more miserable. I suppose he's right, but what I wouldn't give for two minutes with that sorry excuse for a mother.

1

Present day
Last Chance Ranch

So this is the home my mother left more than thirty years ago.

With a sense of foreboding, Rafe Locke turned into the circular gravel drive that fronted a two-story log ranch house, climbed out of his rented Lexus and pocketed the keys. He hoped the car's shocks were okay.

The luxury sedan might not have been the best choice for driving over the rutted dirt road leading to the main house, but trucks were his twin brother Wyatt's style, not his. Wyatt operated a wilderness trekking company and loved long, arduous hikes. Rafe gave financial advice to high-profile clients and worked out at a gym.

Although Wyatt had offered to meet his plane at the Jackson airport, the guy was a busy bridegroom with things to do. And things on his mind, like whether their mother, Diana, would risk returning to face her oldest son, Jack, in order to attend Wyatt's wedding.

Whether Diana showed up or not, Rafe wanted to be

in charge of his own transportation during the week of wedding festivities. Once their dad, Harlan, arrived, he'd also appreciate having the Lexus at his disposal. He didn't like driving trucks, either.

As Rafe surveyed the house with its wide porches and country ambiance, he had no trouble imagining his mother's objections to the lifestyle. The structure represented home and hearth, not the sleek sophistication Diana craved.

She would sneer at the rockers lining the porch and the horseshoe knocker on the massive front door. She'd think the multicolored flower beds on either side of the porch steps lacked design and restraint. She'd hate the wrought-iron boot scraper anchored in cement beside the steps.

The house had quite a bit of square footage, though, and Wyatt had said the acreage was considerable, too. Rafe hoped the Chance family had a good financial advisor. Considering property values in a resort area like Jackson Hole, they were likely sitting on several million in assets.

Wyatt seemed oblivious to that, which was so like him. Instead he'd rattled on about the family history, and how Archie Chance and his bride, Nelsie, had built the center section themselves during the Great Depression. Later two wings had been added at an angle that made them look like arms reaching out to welcome visitors.

Or ensnare them. His mother had said she'd felt trapped at the Last Chance. Escaping to San Francisco and marrying financier Harlan Locke had been her solution. Except her marriage to Harlan had come apart eighteen months ago, and Rafe knew she wouldn't look forward to socializing with her ex, especially when they'd be prominently showcased as the mother and father of the groom.

But that issue paled in comparison to her confronting Jack, the son she hadn't contacted since she'd left, the son who Wyatt, Rafe and Harlan hadn't found out about until after the divorce. Wyatt had chosen to visit the ranch and meet his half brother. He'd discovered that Jonathan Chance, Jack's father and Diana's first husband, had died, but he'd left two more sons, Nick and Gabe, and a widow, Sarah.

Wyatt had fallen in love with Jackson Hole, the Chance family and Olivia Sedgewick. Rafe wished to hell Wyatt had agreed to marry Olivia somewhere else, anywhere else. But she was local and Wyatt wanted the wedding to take place at the ranch, which he considered his new home base.

Rafe suspected Wyatt also had an agenda that included Diana finally making peace with Jack. Wyatt had bonded with his half brother and wanted the old wounds healed. Knowing softhearted Wyatt, he had dreams of the Lockes and the Chances becoming one big happy family.

Although Rafe was also Jack's half brother, he had no such dreams. He'd do his job as best man because he loved his twin, but Wyatt was the outlier in the Locke family. Diana, Harlan and Rafe were dyed-in-the-wool San Franciscans used to their sushi bars and lattes. Whooping it up in cowboy country wouldn't be their idea of a good time.

Thinking of urban conveniences reminded Rafe that he hadn't checked his cell phone reception since turning off the main highway. Monday was a busy trading day and he'd been AWOL for a good part of it. Time to play catch up before he announced his presence to anyone inside.

After tucking his Wayfarer sunglasses in his shirt pocket, he reached inside the car, pulled his iPhone from the holder on the dash and tested the internet connection. Amazingly, it worked.

Absorbed in checking end-of-trading stock prices, he lost track of his surroundings until the sound of rapid hoofbeats made him whirl in alarm. A horse and rider bore down on him. Swearing, he dove into the car to avoid having himself and his iPhone smashed to bits.

Instead of stampeding past, the rider pulled up right next to the car. The horse snorted loudly and stretched its nose toward the Lexus. The beast could be breathing fire and brimstone for all Rafe knew.

"Did I scare you?" The voice was decidedly female. "Sorry about that."

Rafe tossed his phone on the seat and slid carefully out, giving the brown-and-white horse a wide berth. "I wasn't scared. I was startled." He glared up at the rider, whose red hair curled out from under the brim of a brown cowboy hat. "Anybody who sees a horse running straight at him would—"

"Cantering. Spilled Milk and I were just cantering toward you."

"Looked damned fast to me."

"I was trying to catch you before you went inside. I saw the car and realized you must be Rafe, and I wanted to introduce myself." She swung down from the saddle, dropped the reins to the ground and held out her hand. "I'm Meg Seymour, Olivia's maid of honor. We'll be in the wedding together on Saturday."

So this was Meg, and she wasn't at all what he'd expected, but she had a warm, firm handshake. Now that she was on the ground, he estimated her height at around five-eight. The boots added another couple of inches, and the hat a couple more, which made her seem almost as tall as he was.

"I thought you were from Pittsburgh," he said. Wyatt had told him that, and Rafe had held out the vain hope that Meg would be a kindred spirit who wasn't into the jeans and boots routine. Instead, here she was decked out like a certified cowgirl.

"I am from Pittsburgh."

"Have you spent a lot of time out here?" Rafe eyed the horse, which kept stretching its neck toward him as if wanting to take a bite. Rafe edged back.

"Nope. My first time. Hey, don't worry about Spilled Milk. She's just curious. You can rub her nose. She likes that."

"Uh, no thanks." Although he kept his attention on the horse, he managed to get a quick glimpse of Meg's green eyes and the light dusting of freckles across her nose. She was cute enough, but thanks to her he was too damned close to an animal who wanted to eat him. Meg had dropped the reins as if abandoning all responsibility.

She shrugged. "Okay. I guess you're not much into horses."

"Not really. Shouldn't you be holding on to her?"

"She's trained to stand still when I drop the reins."

That was all well and good, but from where the horse stood, she could easily reach him with those big teeth. "Is she trained not to bite?"

"Absolutely, but if she's making you nervous, I can—"

"I'm not nervous, but I don't want to get bit, either." Great. Now he looked like a wuss.

"Let me back her up some." Turning to the horse, she picked up the reins. "Back, girl. That's it. A little more. Good."

Rafe breathed easier, which allowed him to pick up a cinnamon scent that he'd guess belonged to Meg and not the horse. When she'd turned to move the animal back, he also couldn't help noticing the great fit of her jeans. He wasn't into the country look, but snug jeans showed off a woman's ass to good advantage, and hers was worth admiring.

Keeping herself between Rafe and the curious horse, she faced him again. "Better?"

"It's just that I live in the city." That wasn't much of an excuse. She lived in the city and she was totally at ease with this animal. "Where did you learn so much about horses?"

"I'm no expert, but I ride English back home. I had to adjust to a Western saddle when I arrived, but I've about accomplished that, so tomorrow I can start learning how to rope."

"You want to learn to rope this week?"

"I do."

"Why?"

"Because it's something I've never tried and being on the ranch gives me a golden opportunity. I really love it here." She smiled.

And Rafe's breath caught. Earlier he'd thought she was cute with her freckles, her shamrock-green eyes, and her red curls peeking from under her hat, but that smile of hers turned cute into beautiful. Her beauty was all the more impressive because he couldn't see a trace of makeup.

She studied him for a moment. "You know, Wyatt said you didn't look like him, and you sure don't."

"We're fraternal twins, not identical."

"He said that, but still, I expected some similarities. Instead of being on the fair side like Wyatt, you're a *GQ* version of Jack Chance. Same dark hair, same dark eyes. Dress you up in Jack's trademark black shirt, jeans and boots, and you could pass for him."

"I doubt it. There's not an ounce of cowboy in me."

She gave him another once-over. "Then you'll have to fake it for the wedding."

"I'll follow the dress code when I have to, but not until then."

Her eyebrows rose. "You didn't bring jeans and boots?"

"Don't own any."

"Oh, that's no problem. I'm sure you'd fit into Wyatt's clothes, or Jack's for that matter."

The idea of wearing jeans and boots was bad enough, but wearing borrowed jeans and boots was worse. "Thanks, but I really don't need them until the wedding and I'll pick up the required outfit for the ceremony later in the week."

Her look of confusion was almost funny. "But... how can you try riding if you don't have any jeans and boots?"

"I can't, which is fine with me. Wyatt promised me I wouldn't have to get on a horse, and I'm holding him to it."

She stared at him, apparently at a loss for words.

"The thing is, Wyatt and I not only look different, but we have totally different personalities. He's the rugged outdoor type, and I'm the urban professional type. I'm crazy about the guy and wish him well in whatever he does, but we have almost nothing in common."

"Yes, but you're not in San Francisco now. You're *here*. Why wouldn't you want to take advantage of what the Last Chance has to offer?"

A tiny voice in the back of his head murmured *because I don't want to make a fool of myself*. He wasn't ready to acknowledge that voice to himself, let alone to the maid of honor. "Because riding and roping and mucking out stalls, or anything that's involved with ranching, doesn't interest me."

"Then what will you do all day?"

"I have my iPad and my iPhone. When Wyatt doesn't need me for wedding stuff, I'll work remote."

"Ah." She nodded. "He said you're involved in the financial world somehow."

Trust Wyatt to be vague on that point. His twin had never quite grasped what Rafe did for a living. "I'm a financial advisor."

"And I'm sure you're good at it, too."

"I hope so. I have clients who depend on me being good at it." He even managed some investments for Wyatt, who gave him carte blanche to do whatever he thought was right.

Her green gaze became serious. "Please take this next comment in the spirit of friendly advice."

"Okay."

"The Last Chance is an amazing place. In the few days I've been here, I've heard stories of lives being changed by contact with this ranch and the people on it. I'd hate for anyone to waste that privilege."

"Meaning me."

"Yes."

He thought her earnest advice was sweet, even if it was misguided. "The thing is, I don't want my life to change."

"Well, then." She gave him a look filled with pity. "I guess it's a good thing you brought your iPad and iPhone." She mounted up. For a moment she hesitated, clearly still thinking about his response and whether to say anything more. Then her expression closed down. "See you at dinner."

"Sure. Nice meeting you."

"Same here." With a wave, she turned Spilled Milk around and urged the horse toward a large, hip-roofed barn about two hundred yards to the right of the house.

Rafe didn't have to be a mind reader to know that Meg was disappointed in his attitude. But damn it, he hadn't come here to attend cowboy school. Or to change his life.

Most guys would give their eyeteeth to live the way he did. He made decent money, rented an apartment with a view of the bay and dated sexy women. He was only twenty-nine, and although his twin had decided to tie the knot, he felt no similar urge.

After watching his parents' marriage dissolve and the messy financial entanglements of that dissolution, he'd vowed to be very sure before he made a commitment. If he should find the perfect woman in the far distant future, he'd want her to be a successful businesswoman in her own right, someone who was as happy with a San Francisco lifestyle as he was. And there would definitely be a prenup.

In any case, he was in no hurry to get to that stage. He liked his present status just fine, and if Miss Meg Seymour wanted to dive into ranch activities and see about changing *her* life, she was welcome to it. But she could leave him out of that program, thank you very much.

2

MEG FROWNED AT HER REFLECTION in the mirror. She'd tried on every pair of earrings she'd brought to Wyoming, plus the long and dramatic ones in turquoise and silver that she'd bought during a shopping trip in Jackson with Olivia. She'd also changed clothes three times.

This was not like her, and she was angry with herself because she knew the cause of it all. She wanted to look stunning for Rafe Locke when she came down to dinner. What a ridiculous goal that was.

One glance had told her that he dated skinny women in designer dresses and up-to-the-minute hairstyles who had exotic jobs in the art district. That was so not her.

She'd never been skinny or willing to shell out for designer clothes or an expensive salon cut. She was a brainy engineer who worked for the City of Pittsburgh designing traffic-control systems in areas of urban growth. She had her hair cut at the same Pittsburgh salon where her BFF Olivia had worked until a year ago, when she'd moved to Wyoming.

But Rafe had snagged her attention. He claimed not to be interested in ranch life, but she sensed he was more wary than uninterested and possibly afraid of looking foolish doing something he wasn't good at. His apparent reluctance to step out of his comfort zone posed an irresistible challenge to her.

She knew from personal experience that breaking through self-imposed boundaries created a life full of excitement. Rafe's attitude implied that the Last Chance would be a blip on his ultrasophisticated radar, a place to tolerate until he could satisfy his duties as best man and return to the rarified, and possibly stifling, air of his San Francisco existence. Shaking him out of that self-satisfied rut would be good for him and tons of fun for her.

His well-toned body tempted her, too. Those broad shoulders and narrow hips would look great in cowboy gear. She could picture his dark eyes shadowed by a tilted Stetson. Oh, yeah.

At least once during their meeting this afternoon she'd caught a flash of interest in his expression. Building on his initial interest might be a way to lure him into tasting cowboy life. He really did look like a younger version of Jack Chance, and almost every woman in Shoshone agreed that Jack was sexier than hell. He was also taken.

Rafe was not, and he had the makings of a hero. After all, he was Wyatt's twin and Jack's half brother, so a cowboy's soul could be hiding under that urban exterior and just waiting to be turned loose. Meg figured she had first crack at him, at least for the week of the wedding. Wasn't that the prerogative of the maid of honor when the best man was single? If it wasn't in the wedding party rules, it should be.

This dithering had made her late, though. She'd heard

Olivia and Wyatt arrive at least twenty minutes ago and the sound of laughter and the clink of glasses from downstairs told her that drinks were being served in the living room. In late August the weather was nippy enough for a fire in the evenings and she could smell cedar smoke. All the Chance family would gather tonight because welcoming Wyatt's twin, who was also Jack's half brother, was a big deal.

Rafe would be down there trying to keep everyone in the family straight in his mind. Meg felt a little sorry for him having to deal with it after a day of traveling. And he didn't fit into this ranch crowd at all, which wouldn't help.

Meg felt totally comfortable here and had a good memory for names and faces. Even so, she always mentally reviewed the players before jumping into a large gathering. Jack, the oldest Chance son, was married to Josie, who owned the local tavern Spirits and Spurs. Their baby son was named Archie after his great-grandfather.

Next oldest was Nick, a large-animal vet who'd married Dominique, a talented photographer. They were plowing through the paperwork to adopt Lester, a thirteen-year-old boy in foster care who'd been part of a work program for disadvantaged youth held at the ranch for the first time this summer. Nick and Dominique, along with everyone at the ranch, had fallen in love with Lester and had decided they'd be more than happy to start their family with him.

The youngest son, Gabe, was married to Morgan, a redhead. Meg and Morgan had bonded over the joys and problems of having red hair. Morgan and Gabe's little toddler, Sarah Bianca, had inherited the red hair, so Meg felt right at home with those two.

The sixtysomething ranch foreman, Emmett Sterling, would probably be at the gathering because he'd worked at the ranch for years and was considered part of the family. He actually might become part of the family if he and Pam Mulholland, who ran a nearby bed-and-breakfast, ever got married. Pam was Nick Chance's aunt, and she'd be there, too.

Sarah Chance, the matriarch of the group, had finally found a new love after the untimely death of her husband several years ago. Peter Beckett, her fiancé, would be in attendance. A philanthropist, he'd funded the ranch's summer program for young teens.

It was a lot to take in and, unlike Wyatt, Rafe didn't seem eager to embrace the Chance family. That would throw extra tension into a situation already filled with drama.

Meg liked and admired the Chance family, but her personal obligation was to Olivia and Olivia's sweetheart, Wyatt. By extension, Meg felt some loyalty to Rafe, and he'd have a much easier time of it if he'd get that burr out from under his saddle, as they said out here in the West.

"Meg?" Olivia's voice floated down the hall. "I've been sent up to check on you."

"I'm in here." Meg shook her head and made the silver-and-turquoise earrings dance. They went well with the black dress she'd settled on, the simple little black dress that every woman was supposed to have hanging in her closet. Knowing her limitations in the fashion department, Meg had clung to that advice.

Olivia, looking radiant in a dark green dress, appeared in the doorway of what was still referred to as "Roni's room." The Chances had taken Roni in when she was a runaway teen. Now she worked as a mechanic on the NASCAR circuit and had married a guy on her racing team.

The decor hadn't been updated since the days when Roni had been obsessed with NASCAR. But it was the only upstairs bedroom with an attached bath, so it was usually assigned to any single female guest. Meg qualified and was grateful for the privacy.

"Oh, Meg, those earrings are spectacular with that dress." Olivia beamed at her.

"And you look terrific, as always." Meg glanced lovingly at her friend. Olivia constantly experimented with her hair, and recently she'd colored it in various shades of red and blonde. For tonight's event she'd created an arrangement of upswept curls and dangling ringlets that inspired Meg's awe.

"Thank you." Olivia smiled. "Being crazy in love helps."

"I don't have that going for me, unfortunately. I wish I'd asked you to come early and do my hair. It just sits there, a curly red blob."

"Is that what's keeping you?" Olivia crossed to the dressing table, picked up a tube of gel and squeezed some into her palm. "I can fix that in a jiffy."

"The hair, the dress, the makeup, the jewelry. I've been a mass of writhing indecision." Meg's anxiety level dropped significantly as Olivia massaged hair gel into her misbehaving curls.

"Sounds serious." Olivia finished with the gel and picked up a brush and a hair dryer. "You're usually the calmest one of the bunch."

"I think it's having Rafe here."

"He does change the dynamics." She turned the dryer on low and began to work. "He's a different kind of guy and he doesn't quite fit in at the moment, but I'm counting on the fact he's Wyatt's twin. He'll be fine. It'll all work out."

"I hope so. He seems sort of…" Meg hesitated to label him and risk offending his future sister-in-law.

"So you've met him?"

"I introduced myself this afternoon. He thinks I tried to run him down while I was on Spilled Milk."

Olivia met Meg's gaze in the mirror and laughed. "So did you?"

"No! Of course not!"

"Just wondering, because speaking for myself, I have the strongest urge to mess with him."

Meg grinned, relieved she could be honest. "Livy, he's ridiculously uptight. He told me he has 'no interest' in participating in the activities of the ranch. Won't dress in jeans and boots until forced to. Plans to spend the week checking in to work on his iPad. How crazy is that?"

Olivia nodded. "That's what he said just now, too. He seems to be holding the ranch and the Chance family at arm's length. Poor Wyatt doesn't know what to do."

"Well, that sucks. For Wyatt and you, but for Rafe, too. He has no idea what he's missing. It's a crime to come to this beautiful ranch and stay cooped up with an iPad."

"I agree." Olivia used the brush and hair dryer to arrange Meg's hair in soft, layered curls that framed her face. "There, how's that?"

"Incredible." Meg turned her head to view the results. The earrings swung rhythmically as she moved. "Now I feel gorgeous enough to take on Rafe Locke."

Olivia smiled. "And do what with him?"

"You know, I think, deep down, he might *want* to loosen up, but he's afraid to. He needs some help."

"Well, if anyone can help him overcome those fears, it's you." Olivia stood back. "Go get him, girl."

RAFE WAS HOLDING UP, but just barely. The shock of seeing his doppelganger—Jack Chance—walk into the room had largely worn off, but keeping the names and faces of the Chance clan sorted out had taken its toll. Fortunately no one had asked him the million-dollar question—whether Diana was coming to the wedding.

Even if they had, he wouldn't have been able to give them an answer. He realized his mother was taking rudeness to a new level by waiting this long to reply, but surely a family rift that had lasted thirty-two years gave her some dispensation from the Emily Post crowd. He didn't condone her behavior, either now or thirty-two years ago, but he didn't want to see her humiliated, either.

He was trying to figure out a way to ditch the whole dinner plan and head upstairs to bed when Meg walked down the curved staircase looking like a queen at her coronation. He stared, then caught himself and glanced away.

But the image stayed with him. She'd abandoned the cowgirl look for a slinky black dress that showed off cleavage he hadn't imagined existed when she'd worn a T-shirt. Her curly red hair now fell in soft waves around her face, and dangling earrings caught the light as she moved.

Dressed like this, she could walk into any nightclub in San Francisco and turn heads. She was turning them here, even though every man in the place except Rafe was spoken for. After an hour in the company of these guys, Rafe knew they all adored their wives, or fiancée in Wyatt's case. But a man would have to be dead not to notice Meg tonight.

The only male who dared say something was thirteen-year-old Lester, a foster kid who would eventually be a part of the Chance family when Nick and Dominique formally adopted him. Lester gazed up at Meg with reverence in his eyes. "Wow. You clean up real good."

That brought a laugh from everyone, including Meg. "Thanks, Lester." She touched the lapel of the boy's new Western shirt. "You're pretty stylin' yourself."

"This is new." Lester stuck out his skinny chest to show off his shirt. "Boots are new, too. Ropers."

"Very nice. I'll bet you and Nick went shopping today."

Rafe covertly watched the interchange and wished he'd had the presence of mind to compliment her instead of allowing Lester to take the lead. The boy was small for his age, but apparently he had a gift for working with horses. Of the eight boys who'd spent the summer months at the ranch, Lester had been the standout according to Sarah. Nick and Dominique couldn't stop talking about how much they enjoyed having him as part of their family.

Gazing at Lester, Rafe thought about what Meg had said this afternoon about the Last Chance changing lives. Here was a perfect example and Rafe applauded the effort. The ranch was a lifeline for a boy like Lester, but Rafe didn't happen to need saving.

Wyatt walked over to stand beside him. "I saw your reaction when Meg came down, bro." He gestured in her direction with his beer bottle. "It's the most animated you've been since you arrived."

"She's a good-looking woman." Rafe took a sip of his red wine as he watched Meg fuss over Lester.

"She's also really special to Olivia."

Rafe glanced at Wyatt. In the two months since Rafe had last seen him, Wyatt had become a cowboy, both in dress and attitude. It suited him. "That sounded like a warning. Are you saying I should keep my hands off Meg?"

"That's not my place. Meg is a big girl, and she makes her own decisions. I've come to respect that about her. I'm just saying that you shouldn't... Hell, I don't know what I'm saying."

"I do." Rafe usually could tell what his twin was thinking, even if Wyatt couldn't put it into words. "You're telling me not to cause a problem for your fiancée's best friend. I promise not to do that."

"Thanks. I appreciate it." Wyatt squeezed Rafe's shoulder. "Looks like Sarah's herding us all into the dining room. I think you'll enjoy the food."

"I'm sure I will. The ranch is great, Wyatt."

"Yeah, it is." Relief shone in Wyatt's gray eyes. "I'm glad you see that."

Rafe felt like a first-class jerk. He'd known Wyatt desperately wanted his approval of the place and the family. That had been plain ever since Wyatt had announced his engagement. Yet Rafe had been reserving judgment, holding himself slightly apart. As his twin, Wyatt had sensed Rafe's attitude and had been troubled by it.

Rafe would rather cut off his arm than hurt Wyatt, and his behavior was doing exactly that. "I've been thinking," he said as they walked down a hallway lined with family photos. "Maybe I should take a shot at riding a horse while I'm here."

Wyatt laughed. "You don't have to do that, buddy. I know it's not your thing."

"That's true." He remembered what Meg had said this afternoon. "But when am I ever going to have a better setup than this?"

"That's true. I'd take you out tomorrow, except Olivia and I are having a final meeting with the caterers in the morning, and we're double-checking the flower order in the afternoon, but the next day I could probably—"

"Don't worry about it. I'm sure there are a million people around here who could teach me the basics." He immediately thought of Meg, but discarded the idea. She intrigued him far too much, and things could get messy. He'd just promised his brother not to create a problem.

Wyatt nodded. "You're right. I'll check with Emmett. He'll know who has some spare time tomorrow."

"Great. You know, this house is huge."

"It is." He gestured to the large room they'd entered. Although it held four round tables that could each seat eight, they weren't set for dinner. "They use this area at lunch and all the hands eat here along with whatever family members are available."

"Sounds like good PR." On his right, through a set of double doors, was a smaller dining room furnished with one long table, the kind that could be expanded or contracted as needed. Gleaming silverware and faceted goblets sparkled in the light from a hammered metal chandelier.

"It's more than PR," Wyatt said. "It's the way the Chance family does things. There's not a bit of snobbery in them."

Guilt pricked Rafe again. "I'm sure that appeals to you."

"Yeah. Don't get me wrong. I love Mom. But she's a terrible snob. And I hate to say it, but so is Dad."

Rafe sighed. "He is, and damn it, I was acting like a snob when I first got here. I'm sorry about that. It's just so…different from what I'm used to."

"I know." Wyatt grinned at him. "That's why I like it here."

Rafe could tell. He was happy for his twin, and he vowed he would do his best to fit in for the short time he was part of Wyatt's new world. As they all filed into the dining room, he hesitated, unsure of where he was supposed to sit.

Sarah glanced his way. "Rafe, why don't you—"

"He can sit here, Sarah." Meg patted a chair next to her. "We're the two who don't have kids or spouses, so we might as well hang out together."

Sarah looked pleased. "That works."

Rafe took the offered chair. "Thanks." Sitting next to her at dinner wasn't the same as making a play for her, so he felt okay with it. He also thought a polite compliment was in order. "You look really nice."

Her cheeks turned slightly pink. "Thank you. I don't get dressed up very often."

That made him wonder how she earned a living. "Where do you work?"

"I'm an engineer for the city. I specialize in traffic

control." She gazed at him steadily, as if to assess his reaction.

"Huh. I've never met someone who did that." So she had brains, too. She intrigued the hell out of him, and he'd just promised Wyatt not to get involved.

"My job doesn't usually make for fascinating dinner conversation."

He laughed as he unfolded his napkin and laid it in his lap. "Mine, either."

"So what shall we talk about?"

"Well…" He couldn't resist telling her of his latest plan, especially after the way she'd goaded him earlier. "You'll be happy to know I'm going to try riding tomorrow."

Her green eyes grew wide. "You *are?*"

"Yep. I decided that you're right. I'll never have a better chance than now, so why not?"

Her smile dazzled him. "That's fabulous. Congratulations."

"Thanks. I'll probably fall off, but what the hell?"

"You won't fall off."

"I might. I don't know the first thing about riding a horse." He picked up his water glass and took a drink.

"It's easy. What time do you want to start?"

He nearly choked on his water. "Start? What do you mean?"

"I mean, after challenging you to experience life on a ranch, I think it's only fair that I be the one to teach you to ride. The hands are all busy and I'm relatively free. So what time?"

"I—" He cast around for a way out of this. He'd be terrible in the beginning, and he didn't relish the idea of looking bad in front of her.

"I suggest eight-thirty. I'll meet you down at the barn." She smiled again. "You're going to love this, Rafe."

"If you say so." He had plenty of misgivings about having her teach him to ride, but the plan had one positive side. Given his lack of experience with horses, the time spent together had zero chance of being romantic.

3

MEG ARRIVED AT THE BARN ten minutes ahead of schedule the next morning. Rafe hadn't shown up in the kitchen for breakfast or even for a cup of coffee, so maybe he'd blow off this lesson. She hoped not. Teaching him to ride would satisfy several objectives.

Olivia and Wyatt would be much happier if Rafe participated in ranch life instead of staying aloof from it as he'd originally planned. Plus Meg enjoyed pushing people out of their comfort zones, and she wouldn't mind getting to know Rafe better. But she couldn't force him to do this.

If he didn't keep their appointment, she'd back off, way off. She valued those who made agreements and kept them. Anyone who couldn't do that moved several notches down in her estimation.

After petting Butch and Sundance, the two dogs lying on either side of the barn's double door, Meg stepped inside and breathed in the welcome scent of hay, oiled leather and horse. She truly loved it in Jackson Hole, and specifically at this ranch. After only four days, she was already questioning whether she wanted to stay in Pittsburgh or consider a move to Wyoming.

Her two older brothers had moved away, one to Connecticut and the other to Indiana. Although her parents still lived in Pittsburgh, they'd started making plans to retire in Florida. She really had nothing holding her except a job and friends.

The job was no problem. She could find something out here. And her friends would simply come visit. The more she thought about the idea, the more she liked it.

Besides, she was already making friends here, like the foreman, Emmett Sterling. She found him oiling tack, which explained why the tangy scent had been so strong when she'd first come into the barn.

At their initial meeting she'd told him that he reminded her of Tom Selleck, especially with his graying mustache. Emmett had blushed. He was an old-fashioned cowboy, a modest man with a strong work ethic, and she admired that.

He glanced up with a smile when she walked into the barn. "Hey, there. When do you want to schedule that roping lesson?"

"I'm not sure yet, Emmett. I don't know if you've heard that I volunteered to teach Rafe how to ride, assuming he hasn't changed his mind since last night."

"I did hear that from Wyatt." He gave a nod of approval. "Great idea."

"If he comes. Maybe he's decided not to."

Emmett looked over her shoulder. "I think you're in luck."

She turned and tried not to let her jaw drop. For a second she thought Jack had walked into the barn, but the stride was different and the jeans were blue denim, not the black that Jack favored. No telling where Rafe had dug up the jeans, shirt, boots and hat, but they fit him well.

A little too well, in fact. Yesterday his dress shirt and slacks had partially disguised his build, but this outfit disguised nothing. The snug jeans showed off his muscled thighs and the shirt emphasized his broad chest.

The borrowed hat was black. By accident or design, Rafe had tilted it at the right angle to make his dark eyes sexy and mysterious, exactly as she'd imagined they would be when shadowed by a hat. He looked amazing.

He came to a stop in front of her and spread out his arms. "Will this do?"

She had the inappropriate urge to move right into those outstretched arms in the hope he'd wrap them around her. "You should wear clothes like that more often." Whoops. She'd said that out loud. "I mean, yes, that'll do fine."

"Sarah rounded them up for me this morning."

"Did you eat any breakfast? I didn't see you in the kitchen."

"I never eat breakfast. I grabbed a cup of coffee before I came down here. That's all I need."

She didn't think so. He might get away without breakfast when he sat in an office clicking computer keys, but his morning routine was about to shift dramatically toward fresh air and exercise. She decided against mentioning his need for real food because he probably wouldn't believe her.

Instead she turned to the foreman, who was watching them with thinly disguised amusement. "Emmett, which horse do you recommend for Rafe?"

Emmett didn't hesitate. "Destiny."

"I was thinking that, too."

Rafe shifted his weight and looked apprehensive. "'Destiny' sounds like the devil horse you put green-horns on to test them."

"We wouldn't do that, son." Emmett clapped him on the shoulder. "You've come here with an honest desire to learn how to ride. If you'd bragged about your rid-ing skill when we knew you didn't have any, *then* we'd bring out the devil horse."

"Trust me, I have nothing to brag about when it comes to horses. I can deconstruct a stock offering in no time flat, but when it comes to mounting up and rid-ing off into the sunset, I got nothin'."

Emmett reached for a halter hanging on the wall. "It's not a bad place to start. You're a blank slate with no bad habits. Meg, if you want to lead out Spilled Milk, I'll fetch Destiny. Rafe, you come with me. I'll show you how to put this on him."

Meg watched the two men head down the row of stalls. Emmett ambled along with the slightly bow-legged stride of a guy who'd spent most of his life in the saddle. Rafe moved with the grace of an athlete, but there was no cowboy in his walk yet. Even so, the view of a jeans-wearing Rafe from behind was outstanding. Life at the Last Chance had just become more scenic.

DESPITE BEING ASSURED that Destiny wasn't a powder keg ready to explode, Rafe studied the large brown-and-white animal from outside the stall. He wasn't eager to get into a confined space with him.

"Come on in, son. He won't bite."

Rafe edged into the stall. "How much does he weigh?"

"Around a thousand pounds, give or take."

"He must be pretty strong."

"Yes, but he's trained to cooperate with you. Come closer so you can see how to halter him. You put this on in order to lead him out of the barn. Later you'll take the halter off and replace it with a bridle, which provides your steering mechanism. Don't worry. He's used to all this, so he won't put up a fuss."

"Right." Taking a deep breath, Rafe approached Destiny. As Emmett put on the halter, Rafe ignored the enormous teeth and concentrated on Destiny's deep brown eyes. He could see himself in the reflection there, and he *looked* like a cowboy, even if he didn't feel like one.

"See how that's done?" Emmett finished with the halter, snapped a lead rope to a metal ring and handed over the rope. "Go ahead and lead him outside."

Before Rafe could object that he didn't know enough yet, he found himself tramping back down the aisle between the stalls, towing a horse behind him. Emmett walked along, too, probably to make sure Rafe didn't do anything stupid.

"How long has Destiny been at the ranch?"

"Let's see. I guess it's about twenty-four years, now."

"Yikes! I didn't mean you had to give me a geriatric horse. Can he handle my weight?"

Emmett chuckled. "Twenty-four's not so old. Horses can live to be forty or more. Destiny was born when Jack was around ten, and he came up with that name for him. Thought it was real dramatic."

"So this is Jack's horse?"

"Not really. He's a little too tame for Jack these days. Jack rides a black-and-white stallion named Bandit."

"Destiny isn't a stallion?"

"Not anymore."

"Oh." Rafe was torn between relief that Destiny was a pushover and humiliation at being consigned to a horse with no balls, one that wasn't spirited enough for Jack Chance.

"Destiny's a good starter horse," Emmett said. "He has one bad habit, though. If you're out on the trail and decide to climb off him, you'd better tie him up real good. He likes to work himself loose and head on home."

"I'll remember that. But I think maybe I should just stay in the corral today, don't you?"

"Maybe for the first ten minutes, until you get the hang of it."

"I don't think ten minutes will do the trick."

"You'll be surprised at how fast you pick it up, son. Once you're comfortable in the saddle, you and Meg should take 'em out and admire the scenery. We have a lot to look at around here."

"Yes, you do." Rafe couldn't argue with that. Coming out of the house this morning he'd been greeted with a spectacular view of the snowcapped Grand Tetons. Funny that his mother hadn't mentioned the amazing scenery when she'd described the ranch. Lining rockers up on the front porch made a lot more sense when a person could sit and look at those mountains.

When they emerged from the barn, Meg was already at the hitching post with her horse, the one he remembered from yesterday.

"Just tie Destiny up next to Spilled Milk," Emmett said. "I'll get you a blanket, saddle and bridle."

"Thanks, Emmett." Rafe walked the horse in a semi-circle so he could approach the hitching post from the right angle and do a decent job of parallel parking next to the other horse.

After tying the lead rope to the post, he stepped back. "So far, so good."

Meg settled a patterned blanket over her horse's back and glanced at Rafe. "Looks like you and Destiny are making friends."

"I figure he's just putting up with me."

"Just think of him like one of those dogs over there." Moving with calm efficiency, she put a saddle on top of the blanket. "Emmett said he was treated like a pet when he was young, so in some ways he's more dog than horse."

"If I'd ever had a dog, I could relate to that analogy."

"You've never had a dog?"

"Nope."

"You don't like them?" She leaned to tighten the leather strap running under the horse's belly.

"I don't know if I do or not. We didn't have dogs when I was a kid, so I never got used to having them around. With my work schedule, it makes no sense to have a pet, anyway."

"I know what you mean about that. I decided not to adopt a dog right now, either, considering the hours I work. I have a fish tank, but it's not the same. I get my horse and dog fix when I go out to the stables back in Pittsburgh."

She straightened and pointed to the strap under the horse. "It's a good idea to tighten it, then wait for the horse to let out some air, then tighten it again."

"Good to know."

"Okay, now I'll tighten it again." She went back to

her task, which gave him a chance to watch her without her being aware.

This morning she'd returned to her cute and wholesome look. Knowing that she could be all sunshine and daisies during the day and transform into a seductress at night fired his blood. He wondered which persona she'd have naked. Probably both.

"Rafe?" Emmett tapped him on the shoulder. "You okay?"

Rafe turned toward him. "I'm fine. Why?"

"I told you a couple of times that I'd brought out your tack, but you were staring into space like you didn't hear me."

"Sorry." He tugged his hat lower and hoped Emmett wouldn't notice his embarrassment. "Lost in thought, I guess."

Emmett's slow smile indicated he knew exactly where Rafe's mind had been. "Be careful," he said in a low voice.

"I will." He knew neither of them were talking about horseback riding. Meg had at least two male protectors, and Rafe wouldn't be surprised to find more. She'd made friends in the short time she'd been here, and they didn't want her to get hurt.

Well, neither did he. Wyatt knew that he wasn't in the habit of treating women poorly, but Emmett couldn't know that. In any case, Rafe would leave well enough alone when it came to Meg. Yes, she intrigued him, but pursuing that interest wasn't worth the risk.

"I'll leave you both to carry on with the program," Emmett said. "Holler if you need any help, though."

"Thanks, Emmett," Meg said. "We should be fine."

Giving her horse one last pat, she walked over to Destiny. "Let's get this guy saddled. I'll let you do it."

"All right." Rafe put the blanket on the way she had. Then he made sure the stirrups and the leather belt thing were lying on top of the saddle before he swung it up to Destiny's broad back.

"Good job. You must have been watching very closely."

"I was." Good thing she didn't know how closely.

"Then cinch it up."

"With the belt thing?"

"Yes. It's called a cinch."

"Good to know." He managed to knock his hat in the dirt while he dealt with the cinch.

She picked up his hat, dusted it off and hung it on the saddle. "This hat doesn't have a string to hold it on."

"No. Sarah mentioned that." He grappled with the leather cinch while Destiny stomped his front foot. That startled him, but he soldiered on as if he had no thoughts of that hoof crushing his skull like a melon. "Can horses smell fear?"

"Why, are you afraid?"

"No, no. Just wondered."

"I'm sure they can tell when someone's afraid of them. Then they try to take advantage."

"They do?" He managed to get the cinch buckled and stood up again. "Like how?"

"Like not minding you, walking you under a tree branch to scrape you off, things like that."

"Good thing I'm not afraid of this horse, then." And by God he wouldn't be. He didn't relish the idea of being knocked off by an overhanging branch. "Now we wait for him to let out air, right?"

"Right." Meg gazed at him. "I'm trying to imagine growing up without animals in the house. We had dogs, cats, gerbils, hamsters, you name it. Was someone in your family allergic?"

"No. We had very expensive furniture and my mother didn't want it ruined."

"Ah." For a brief moment sympathy flashed in her green eyes. Then she glanced away, as if she knew that he wouldn't appreciate seeing that emotion coming from her.

She was right. He didn't want her sympathy. "It was more of a hardship for Wyatt than for me. I didn't really feel deprived."

"I guess it's all in what you're used to."

"Exactly. So is it time to tighten the cinch on this hay-burner?"

She laughed in surprise. "*Hay-burner?* Where'd you get that, from some old Western?"

"Probably. It just popped into my head. Hanging out at the old homestead must be affecting my vocabulary."

"Next thing you know you'll be saying things like 'howdy, partner' and 'don't you fret, little lady.'"

"God, I hope not. If you hear me start saying dorky things like that, give me a kick, okay?"

"I will." She grinned at him. "And I won't be the only one. Cowboys don't talk like that in real life."

"Do they say 'hay-burner'?"

"They might, among themselves." She leaned closer and lowered her voice. "But if I were you, I'd avoid that one, too. The Chances are proud of their breeding program and their registered Paints. They might be offended."

"Point taken." He savored the cinnamon scent that

wafted from her skin when she was this close. Her mouth looked delicious, and that's why he had to move back and forget about it. He put distance between them, but forgetting about her pink mouth wasn't so easy.

He cleared his throat. "So, is it time to tighten the cinch on this valuable registered Paint?"

"Yes." Her green eyes sparkled. "But Destiny isn't valuable to the horse breeding operation anymore, now that he's no longer—"

"In possession of his family jewels?"

"You noticed?"

"I'm not that observant. Emmett told me. Damned shame."

"It makes him easier to pair up with other horses. Stallions can get touchy with each other, and a mare like Spilled Milk, if she happened to be in season, couldn't go on a trail ride with a stallion. Things could get complicated."

And now he had a visual that was no help in getting his mind off sex. "I hadn't thought of all that."

"Fortunately, Emmett and I did. So cinch him up, and we'll get started."

"Sure thing." Rafe was able to pull the cinch a couple of notches tighter, and while he did, he thought about the poor horse's missing sexual equipment. Rafe, however, wasn't missing any of his, and whenever he looked at Meg, his animal instincts took over.

He'd been so sure a riding lesson couldn't possibly become sexual in nature. Less than thirty minutes into the session, it already had.

4

MEG WONDERED IF RAFE had been warned not to get too friendly with her. Wyatt might have done that, and although she appreciated his big-brother, protective attitude, she didn't want him discouraging Rafe. Maybe he hadn't, but Meg thought someone had issued a word of caution.

Her attempts to flirt with Rafe would spark an initial response, but then he'd tamp it down. Once they were out on the trail and away from anyone who might overhear, she'd ask him why. Maybe he had his own reasons for putting on the brakes, but she was willing to bet Wyatt was at the bottom of it.

First things first, though. She had to get him comfortable with riding so he'd agree to take one of the ranch's many trails. Each one was beautiful, and Meg could hardly wait to show Rafe the wonders he'd been willing to dismiss yesterday.

When Destiny was saddled, she had Rafe watch her put on Spilled Milk's bridle. Then she helped him with Destiny's and explained how the bit worked to control the horse. Finally it was time for Rafe to mount up.

"You get on from the left side." She took his hat off the saddle horn and handed it to him. "You'll want the saddle horn available to hold on to while you swing up."

"Got it." He settled the Stetson on his head and instantly added a yummy factor.

She hadn't realized how sexy cowboy hats were until she'd traveled to Wyoming, where it was the headgear of choice. Now she couldn't imagine men choosing to wear anything else. Put a Stetson on a guy and his hottie quotient shot up a good twenty points.

Standing by Destiny's head, she held the horse's bridle while Rafe shoved his booted foot into the left stirrup and swung his right leg over the saddle with natural grace. Once he conquered his initial nervousness, he'd be great at this. And he rocked the denim look. Watching him mount up, which stretched the material in fascinating places, brought a little shiver of delight.

"And just like that, you're on," she said.

"So I am." Gripping the horn with both hands, he shifted in the saddle. "This isn't too bad."

"I need to adjust the stirrups, though. Your legs are longer than the previous rider's. I don't want your knees drawn up like a jockey's."

"Shouldn't I do the adjusting?"

"It'll be more efficient if I do it while you're in the saddle." She was just the girl to adjust his stirrups, too. Considering how close she'd have to be to his muscled thighs, she wouldn't delegate this job to anyone. Moving to his left side, she glanced up. "Take your left foot out of the stirrup."

He obeyed, and as she lifted the flap of leather to alter the length, she savored the flex of muscles beneath the faded jeans. The scent of minty soap, freshly washed denim and pure masculinity swirled around her in a heady combo. She would adjust Rafe's stirrups any day.

"Now the other side." Rounding the back of the horse, she repeated the motion on his right stirrup. "Okay, put your feet in and let's see."

"It feels better."

"Looks better, too. Stand up in them so I can see how much clearance you have." As he did that, she was obliged to gaze at his crotch. Mercy. "Good. You can sit again." She resisted the urge to fan her face.

"I didn't realize there was so much to the fit of the saddle and the stirrups."

"You need to be as comfortable as possible." She didn't want any of that valuable equipment getting bruised, either. Yowza. With an effort she pulled her mind away from the subject of Rafe's endowments. "You'll want to keep your heels down with your weight sinking into them to lower your center of gravity."

"Sarah convinced me to wear the boots because she said the heels would keep my feet from slipping through the stirrups. I decided I didn't want to be dragged to my death, so I went with the boots."

"You won't be dragged to your death, Rafe. I'll save you before that happens."

He smiled at her. "What a relief. I could have worn my loafers, then."

"'Fraid not. The leather shank keeps your shins from chafing. Boots aren't only for impressing women. They serve a purpose."

"Women are impressed with boots?"

"Some are." She untied Destiny's reins from the hitching post.

"Are you?"

She glanced back at him. "Depends whose feet are in them."

He nodded. "Fair enough."

"I thought we'd start by making a few circuits of the corral." She led Destiny over to the gate.

"Please tell me you're not going to lead me around like a kid on a pony ride."

"Just until I get you inside the corral. After all, it is your first time."

"You make me sound like a damned virgin."

That made her laugh. "Would you rather we started out with a wild gallop across the meadow?"

"No, I wouldn't. But I hope nobody sees this part. It's embarrassing."

"It'll be over before you know it." She unlatched the gate, led Destiny inside and latched the gate again. "Ready to take over?"

"I'm so ready."

Knotting the reins, she lifted them over Destiny's head and handed them to Rafe. "Hold these in your left hand, and keep them fairly loose. You don't want to pull on his mouth. He neck reins, so when you want him to go left, lay the reins against the right side of his neck, and vice versa." She stepped back.

Horse and rider remained stationary as Destiny quietly waited for directions.

Rafe frowned. "Where's the gas pedal?"

She realized he really had *no* idea how to ride a horse. Most people knew how to get them going at least. "Nudge him in the ribs with your heels."

He applied a slight pressure.

"Harder."

When he used more force, Destiny started off.

"Remember, reins against the right side of his neck to go left, and against the left side to go right."

"Got it." Rafe followed her instructions, and soon he was controlling Destiny's slow progress around the corral.

"Bored yet?"

"Getting there. How do I speed him up?"

"You nudge him again and click your tongue. But first sink down into your heels, because a trot is—" He was into the trot before she could finish the sentence.

He bounced uncontrollably in the saddle, lost his stirrups, his hat and his temper. He began to swear.

She struggled to keep a straight face. "Pull back gently on the reins and say 'whoa.'"

He did, and sat there catching his breath. "That was torture. What did I do wrong?"

She was impressed that he'd ask the question instead of blaming either her or the horse. "You got ahead of me. A trot isn't an easy gait to master."

"No shit." He climbed down off the horse.

"Are you giving up?" She couldn't believe it, but everyone had a different tolerance for frustration.

"Hell, no, I'm not giving up." Taking hold of Destiny's bridle, he started off at a brisk walk. "Gotta get my hat."

"Oh." She smiled to herself. She'd suspected he might have the makings of a cowboy. And sure enough, he did.

AFTER THAT DEBACLE, RAFE listened more carefully to Meg's instructions, and eventually he began to sense the rhythm of the trot. He still bounced a little, but he didn't lose his stirrups or his hat, which was progress.

Next she taught him to canter around the perimeter of the corral.

He remembered the term *canter* from yesterday. When he'd accused her of running straight at him, she'd protested that she was only cantering. Now he understood why riders would want to do that. He could canter all day long.

"That's good!" she called out. "I think you're ready for the outside world."

He thought so, too. To his surprise, the corral had started to feel confining. He wouldn't claim to be a natural at riding, but he'd caught on a lot faster than he'd expected.

Meg opened the gate. "Wait here by the corral while I get Spilled Milk. Then we'll be off." She gazed up at him. "You're doing great. Really wonderful for your first time. How do you feel?"

"Terrific." It was the God's truth. He'd ridden motorcycles, but this was better, more…real. He liked the view from the back of a horse, the sense of partnership he felt, and the visceral thrill of going fast in tandem with this powerful animal.

"You'll be sore tomorrow, but maybe not too bad. I recommend a soak in a hot bath later on."

"I'll do that. You haven't led me astray so far."

"Give me time." She winked at him and sauntered away.

What the hell? He stared after her, his brain buzzing with what had obviously been a suggestive remark. And in case he'd been too dense to pick up on it, she'd followed it with a wink.

Digging his cell phone out of his jeans pocket, he speed-dialed his brother.

Wyatt answered immediately. "What's up, bro?"

"What if Meg has the hots for me?"

"She does?"

"I think she might, yeah."

Wyatt let out a gusty sigh. "Figures."

"Look, I don't want to cause— Whoops, gotta go. Here she comes." He disconnected and shoved the phone back in his front pocket. He'd thought of leaving it behind, but the jeans fit tight enough that he wouldn't lose it, and he was used to having his phone with him at all times.

Her eyes narrowed as she approached on Spilled Milk. "Keeping up with stock prices?"

With a sense of shock, he realized that he hadn't thought of his job once since waking up this morning. Normally he'd have checked the market several times by now. "No. I had to ask Wyatt about something."

The disapproval faded from her green eyes. "Best man stuff?"

"Yeah, kind of."

"I know the preparations are important, but could I ask you a big favor?"

"Sure."

"Would you mind turning off your phone during the ride? We have a bright, sunny day to enjoy some gorgeous scenery. I hate to think of it being interrupted by a cell phone chime."

"I can do that." He took out the phone and noticed there was a text message from Wyatt. He'd read it later. Turning off the power, he tucked the phone away again.

"Thank you."

"You're welcome." He met her gaze. Her eyes glowed with happy anticipation. She was looking forward to this ride, looking forward to spending time alone with him. Wyatt and Emmett might be worried about a potential involvement, but she seemed to have no such fears.

He allowed himself to imagine what it would be like to kiss her, and fire licked through his veins. Wyatt had said she was a big girl who made her own choices, and for some reason, she'd chosen a private ride.

Unless he was mistaken, and he rarely was when it came to a woman's interest, she was giving him the green light. Only a fool would ignore that kind of opportunity. Rafe's body warmed to the possibilities as his expectations shifted. He was no fool.

"I'll lead because I know the path, but if you have any problems at all, sing out. I'll keep tabs on you from time to time."

He grinned. "To make sure I'm not being dragged to my death?"

"Yeah, stuff like that. Let's ride." Turning Spilled Milk, she started away from the barn at a brisk trot.

Rafe enjoyed the sight of her ass rising and falling in sync with her horse. Although he was glad she wasn't babying him, he hoped the entire ride wouldn't be a trotting marathon. He still bounced. Even with the bouncing, though, he was filled with elation at the prospect of riding out into the open field…and what might follow once they were truly all alone.

The sun warmed his shoulders and the mountains thrust pristine white peaks into a sky so blue it looked painted on. To think he'd planned to spend the day working. Tightness in his chest that he hadn't realized was there began to loosen.

They stopped briefly so Meg could deal with a gate that led to the wide-open spaces.

"Do you know if all of this is Chance land?" he asked as she leaned down from her horse to fasten the gate behind them.

"Yes, it is." She moved past him so she was once again in the lead. "Archie Chance won it in a card game in the thirties."

"That sounds like a myth. Things like that don't really happen."

"I guess they do in Wyoming. Ready for some cantering?"

"You know it."

"Then let's go!" She urged her horse forward.

Destiny didn't need any nudging as he set off in pursuit of Spilled Milk. A gust of wind nearly took Rafe's hat, and he used one hand to anchor it. At first he held the reins and the saddle horn with his other hand, but as his body adjusted to the horse's rhythm, he let go of the horn and held the reins like a real cowboy would.

He was riding! If he hadn't been worried about spooking the horses, he'd have let out a whoop of delight. What a rush. He couldn't believe he'd gone twenty-nine years without experiencing this. Sharing it with a sexy woman like Meg made it even better.

Before he was ready for the canter to be over, she slowed her horse, and Destiny fell back to a trot, and eventually a walk.

"That was fun," he said. "I could do that again."

"I'm sure you could." She swiveled in her saddle to glance back at him. "But I don't want to overdo it on your first ride. You might feel great now, but you could end up being miserable tonight."

"If I recover okay tonight, do you think we could come out here again tomorrow?"

She smiled at him. "So you really like it that much?"

"Yeah. It's much better than I imagined it would be."

"So maybe you're not totally a city boy."

He shook his head. "I'm still a city boy. Just because I'm enjoying the hell out of this doesn't mean I wouldn't like to find a coffee shop over the next hill."

"No coffee shop. Are you getting hungry?"

He hesitated to admit it after announcing that he never ate breakfast. "A little."

"We can go back."

"Not yet." No way was he going back until he'd had a chance to find out exactly what that wink of hers signified.

"Then we'll keep going." She faced forward again. "It is spectacular, isn't it? According to Sarah, the wildflowers will be gone soon. By September or October, they could have snow."

"I know Wyatt didn't want to wait any later to have the wedding because he was worried about weather."

"I'd like to see this place in the winter. I'll bet it's beautiful then, too. A different kind of beauty."

"Do you ski?" Walking the horses wasn't as exciting, but it meant he could talk to her, get to know her better.

"Not yet. I plan to learn. Olivia wants me to come out here again, so if I visit her this winter, I could learn then. Do you ski?"

"Some. I haven't done it much lately, though. I always seem to be working." The comment made him sound like a drudge, and he wasn't. But he owed it to his clients to keep up with the markets and emerging trends. That required constant vigilance. Today was a rare break in his routine.

"Jackson Hole is a fantastic place to ski."

"So I hear. Wyatt's already said something about celebrating Christmas here, but I don't know…"

"We could visit at the same time and you could teach me to ski! That would be a nice trade, don't you think?"

"It would." So now she was suggesting that they coordinate visits. If that wasn't an indication of interest, then he knew nothing about women.

He liked the prospect of seeing her again in December. He liked it quite a bit, assuming he could do some work while he was here. Many of his clients were shifting assets around at the end of the year, so he was usually busy.

"Of course, there's always the possibility I'll be living here by then."

"Living here?" He had trouble keeping up with her whirlwind approach to life. "You'd move?"

"I'm seriously considering it. I've fallen in love with the area. All I need is a job. Shoshone's a one-traffic-light town, but Jackson might be able to use me in some capacity."

"And you've been here how long?"

"Four days. Five counting today."

"Don't you think you need more time before making a major decision like that?"

She shrugged. "Not really. I grew up in Pittsburgh, and I like it okay, but something about this area just feels like home, you know?"

"Not exactly." He'd never thought in those terms. His parents' house had been a showplace, but not what he'd call a *home*. His own apartment worked for him and had that outstanding view, so he supposed it was home, although he'd never called it that.

"Well, my philosophy is that life's short. You have to grab the good stuff while you can. Speaking of that, there's a pretty little creek up ahead. Let's stop and rest awhile. I didn't think to bring water, so the horses can get a drink and so can we."

"Okay." He tried to decide if he was dealing with a certified flake. Meg was fun to have around and he was sexually attracted to her, but if she'd pull up stakes and switch locations in the blink of an eye, then…then so what? Did it matter?

Even if they got cozy with each other during the week of the wedding, it would be a no-strings affair. Her life decisions wouldn't affect him in the slightest, except that if she moved, she'd be around in December if he made the trip back to Jackson Hole.

But who knew if they'd even like each other at the end of the week if they did become involved. They'd only met yesterday. There might be strong chemistry between them, but until he'd at least kissed her… He almost laughed at his typical caution. Kissing her would be outstanding, and he damned well knew it. The sex would be even better.

Meg pulled her horse to a stop beside a bubbling rivulet of water about two yards wide. "There's a flat rock over there we can sit on."

He liked the idea of the rock, but not the lack of trees. "There's nothing to tie the horses to. Don't forget that Destiny likes to wander."

"I haven't." She dismounted and led her horse to the stream. "But Spilled Milk is trained to be ground-tied, which means if I drop the reins to the ground, she won't go anywhere, so if we tie Destiny's reins to Spilled Milk's saddle horn, we're golden."

"Sounds good." He was perfectly willing to bow to her expertise, especially if it meant being able to spend some time with her on that rock. He felt a few twinges in his muscles as he climbed down. Too bad the ranch didn't have a hot tub on the property, one he could share with Meg tonight.

Copying her actions, he led Destiny over to the water and watched the horse plunge his nose into it. "Here we are watering our horses, just like a scene out of a Western movie."

"Fortunately I don't expect any bad guys to ride up and ambush us."

"If they did, I'd save you. You may know riding, but I know karate." He hadn't practiced in a while, though, so he was glad he wouldn't be put to the test.

She glanced over at him. "We are so trading lessons. I want to learn karate."

"It takes years."

"Oh, I know. I'm not expecting to become an overnight expert, but you could get me started and I could go from there."

"Is there anything you don't want to do?"

"Yes. I don't want to miss anything."

He gazed at her as that statement hovered between them. Did she include him in it? He hoped she did.

She might be a flake, but she was a fascinating one. He'd never met anyone who had such a voracious appetite for life's many experiences. Her enthusiasm was contagious. He'd smiled and laughed more this morning than he had in the past month. If she treated sex the way she did everything else, he was about to become a very lucky man.

5

MEG SENT RAFE OVER TO SIT on the sun-warmed rock while she tied Destiny and Spilled Milk together. Theoretically her plan should work, but she hadn't dealt with Destiny's little quirk. She'd make sure to keep an eye on the horses so she could stop them if they began to wander off.

Once she'd finished, she left the horses and joined Rafe. "Have you had any of the water yet?"

He smiled at her. "I was waiting to see how you planned on doing it. Maybe you're going to drink out of your hat. That's how it's done in the movies."

"I'd rather not." She made a face. "Sounds unsanitary and might ruin my hat." She dropped to her knees. "I'll just scoop it up in my hands, like this." She proceeded to demonstrate the technique she'd used last time she was here.

She'd forgotten that she'd dripped water down the front of her shirt in the process. When she'd been alone it hadn't mattered. She'd sat in the sun until it dried.

But today she was not alone. With an audience making her self-conscious, she got some of the water into her mouth, but most of it ran down her chin and soaked her shirt. She didn't have to look to know that it was plastered to her body and her nipples stood out in sharp relief. She could feel them tightening from the cold.

"Interesting." His voice vibrated with laughter.

"I didn't mean to do that." Winking and flirting was one thing. Setting herself up as a wet T-shirt model was a little over-the-top, even for her. She pulled her shirt away from her body, but the minute she let it go, it clung to her breasts like plastic wrap.

"I'm not complaining."

She cast him a sideways glance, and sure enough, he was frankly admiring her breasts. "A gentleman wouldn't look."

He shoved his hat back with his thumb in a very cow-boylike gesture. "I never claimed to be a gentleman. Besides, weren't you the one who wanted a chance to lead me astray?"

She swallowed. Yes, she'd thought she was quite clever to make that flippant, offhand remark. But now that they were completely alone, she felt the full force and heat of his sexuality. He was one potent guy. She might have bitten off more than she could chew.

Keeping his gaze locked with hers, he took off her hat and laid it on the rock beside her. Then he put his next to it.

Her heart thundered. "Don't you...want a drink of water?"

"I think you scooped enough for two of us." Cupping her cheek in one hand, he leaned forward, his attention on her mouth. "Let's see."

Closing her eyes, she waited, quivering, for what she

guessed would be one of the most outstanding kisses of her life. She wasn't disappointed.

He touched down lightly, sipping the moisture from her lips. His tongue traced the outline once, and again, more slowly. He cradled the back of her head with his other hand and held her still as he continued to explore the contours of her mouth with calm deliberation.

His leisurely approach was at complete odds with her wildly beating heart and the coiled tension she felt coming through his fingertips. She envisioned a small flame licking its way along a fuse to a stick of dynamite.

His breath caught and he swore softly as he pulled back.

Opening her eyes, she looked into the inferno raging in his. "Rafe?"

"You scare the hell out of me."

Dazed by the emotions swirling between them, she could barely speak. "Why?"

"Because I want you so much." With that, he captured her mouth with a ferocity that made her gasp.

Gone was the easy, unhurried caress, the almost lazy attention to her lips. Something raw and primitive seemed to drive him as he thrust his tongue deep with a moan of frustrated desire. She clung to his broad shoulders to keep her balance as the world began to spin.

Her response built quickly. Joy surged within her as she drank in his passion. At last. A man who matched her intensity. He kissed her with the kind of single-mindedness she'd always dreamed of and had never found.

The world narrowed to this connection. Nothing else mattered but kissing Rafe, drawing a quick breath, and kissing him some more. He was ambrosia and nectar of the gods. He was skydiving and parasailing. He was shooting the rapids in a bright red kayak. She couldn't get enough of his mouth, his tongue...

A loud whinny threw her right out of the sensual pool she'd been drowning in. Pulling back, she glanced over at the horses about the time Spilled Milk whinnied again and bared her teeth at Destiny. The gelding was up to his old tricks of trying to walk away, and Spilled Milk was having none of it.

Meg leaped up. "We need to separate them before she completely loses her cool. You untie Destiny while I calm Spilled Milk." She ran over to the horses without waiting to see if Rafe had followed.

Fortunately, he was right behind her. "What happened?" he asked as he untied Destiny's reins from Spilled Milk's saddle.

"I'm guessing that Destiny's been tugging on her and trying to get her to leave. Spilled Milk, being a well-trained horse, stood her ground. The more he pulled, the madder she got. She wasn't going to let him lead her astray."

"As I was trying to do to you?"

She looked over at him and smiled as she stroked the mare's neck. He was one yummy guy. "You could never lead me where I don't want to go, cowboy."

He glanced up. "You do realize that Wyatt warned me to stay away from you."

"I was afraid he'd made me off-limits."

Rafe finished untying Destiny, but he kept a firm grip on the reins. "He told me how special you are, which is something I can see for myself. He seemed to be afraid that I'd somehow cause you problems."

"How?"

He shrugged. "The usual, I suppose. Make passionate love to you and then leave you to cry your eyes out."

"Wyatt's a little too old-fashioned." She held his gaze. "I'm capable of making passionate love without the crying-my-eyes-out routine."

His expression grew serious. "Just so we're both clear on this, I'm not ready to settle down."

"So what? I'm not ready to settle down, either."

"Does Wyatt know that?"

That made her chuckle. "I haven't discussed my relationship plans with Wyatt. I met him for the first time four days ago."

"And yet you're discussing them with me, and you only met me yesterday."

"That's because you could become intimately involved with those plans."

Desire flashed in his eyes. "Are you saying you're fine with a wild and crazy fling this week, with no promises on either side?"

"That's what I'm saying." She mentally crossed her fingers. She might have finally found a man with the same capacity for joy that she had. She never would have guessed it, given his attitude when she'd first met him, but that kiss…that kiss had told her all she needed to know.

If, under his businessman's exterior, Rafe was the kind of passionate man she believed him to be, then she wouldn't easily let him ride off into the sunset. If he truly wanted that, she'd let him go. But as he'd discovered with horseback riding, he might not know exactly what he wanted…yet.

THEIR SIZZLING KISS HAD shaken Rafe more than he cared to admit. He wasn't exactly a novice at this sexual adventure business, but he'd never experienced a first kiss that was quite so explosive. If they could generate that kind of heat with only a kiss, he wondered what would happen when they got down to serious business. He might want to keep a fire extinguisher handy.

He tried to keep his tone casual. "As it happens, we're both sleeping on the second floor, right down the hall from each other."

"Very convenient."

"I think that kind of proximity is what Wyatt was worried about."

Meg seemed to consider that for a moment. "So do you think he's worried about me getting hurt, or could he be worried about our drama interfering with the wedding?"

"Both, probably." Rafe sighed. "The situation's dicey enough without you and me adding to the tension. Everybody's concerned about whether my mother will come to the wedding, which would create one kind of problem, or whether she'll refuse to come, which would create another. Wyatt's in for it, either way."

"Yeah." She nodded as if she'd had the same thoughts. "Do you think we can have what we want without jacking up the drama quotient?"

"I'd like to believe we can." He met her gaze. "Or more accurately, I *want* to believe we can, because… you turn me on, Meg."

"Likewise." Those green eyes told him she was as eager as he was to find out what kind of magic they could create.

He grinned. "That does wonders for a man's ego."

"You're pretty good for mine, too."

"So are you ready to risk it?"

"I am. Are you?"

"With you sleeping right down the hall, I don't know if I could resist the temptation. Maybe I just need to hoist the white flag right now and say I need you in my bed."

"So it's to be your bed, then?" She gave him a teasing glance. "Are you saying you prefer a king-size mattress to a double bed in a room covered with posters of studly NASCAR drivers?"

"I could ignore the posters, but mine is definitely the party bed."

"Okay, so that much is settled. What about…"

He cleared his throat. "Don't worry. I'll take care of that."

"Don't assume you have to. I don't believe a man has to be in charge of birth control. I can run into town this afternoon and make that purchase. I'll just need to know the size."

He couldn't believe how adorable she was. "Ginormous." When her eyes widened, he couldn't help laughing. "What do you suppose a man will say when you ask him a question like that? Of course he'll tell you to get the supersize ones."

"Yes, but I wouldn't want them to fall off."

He laughed harder. "The way they're constructed, I doubt they would, but I'm going to save you the trouble of standing at the counter puzzling over which ones. I know exactly what I want, and what size, so I'm the logical person to take care of that little matter."

Her eyes sparkled. "Or big matter, as the case may be."

"The *huge* matter."

"Okay, okay, I get the idea." She hesitated. "Are we

going to text each other once we're both upstairs, or what?"

"Tell you what. You recommended a hot bath for me, right?"

"Yes."

"When you hear the water running in the bathtub, you're welcome to wander down the hall and scrub my back." Or whatever else she wanted to put her hand to... He shifted his weight as his jeans' fly started to pinch.

"So everything's planned."

"Yep." Rafe made sure he had a good hold on Destiny's reins as he walked around his horse, which was blocking access to Meg. "So Spilled Milk won't move no matter what, right?"

"That's right."

"Good. Then hold these." He put Destiny's reins in her hand.

"How come?"

"I need one more for the road." Sweeping off his hat, he pulled her close and gazed into her green eyes. "Don't let go."

"Rafe Locke, are you about to be a bad boy?"

"Yes, ma'am, I am." Dipping his head below the brim of her hat, he settled his mouth firmly over hers, and once again, the world caught fire.

Except this time the flames licked through his entire body as she wound both arms around his neck and pressed against him. Sweet heaven. He deepened the kiss and she arched forward, sending her hat sliding down her back.

With a groan he cupped her bottom and brought her as close to his aching cock as layers of denim would allow. The dampness from her shirt seeped into his, reminding him of the way her breasts had looked outlined by wet fabric.

Operating with blind desperation, he managed to hook his hat on her horse's saddle so he'd have his other hand free...free to slide under her shirt and cradle her breast in one hand. She shivered and moaned softly.

He longed for bare skin, but now was not the time. Stroking his thumb over damp lace, he caressed her taut nipple as he thrust his tongue deep into her mouth. Tonight. Tonight he'd know the full wonder of making love to her. And it would be so good. So very good.

One of the horses snorted, bringing him back to reality. He lifted his mouth from hers. "Tonight."

"Yes."

What a sweet word that was. He wanted to hear her say it over and over while he gave her all the pleasure she could stand. Groaning, he released her. Tonight. Somehow he'd find the patience to wait until then.

6

MEG'S SHIRT WAS DRY BY the time they brought the horses in, but her pulse still skyrocketed every time she glanced at Rafe. Several of the hands were working around the barn, cleaning stalls and grooming horses, so she didn't look at Rafe very often as they unsaddled Destiny and Spilled Milk, because she didn't want to give herself away.

She showed Rafe how to use a brush on Destiny's glossy coat and they worked side by side, grooming their mounts. Every accidental, or not-so-accidental touch sent a jolt of sexual awareness through her. Rafe was probably affected, too, but he acted totally calm.

"Perfect morning for a ride," he said conversationally. "Couldn't have been better."

A devil took possession of her tongue. "I don't know. I thought it was a little warm out there."

He coughed and cleared his throat. "Personally, I like it on the hot side."

"Then you'll be pleased to know it will stay that way while you're here."

"I'll admit that makes me a happy man. Nothing like working up a sweat doing what you enjoy."

He'd turned the tables on her quite effectively, and now she could barely breathe as she imagined what would happen in that big bed upstairs tonight.

"You're awfully quiet over there, Meg. Cat got your tongue?"

She did her best to calm her racing heart. "I...uh... just remembered I have some things to do up at the house." She put the brush into a bucket and untied her horse from the hitching post. "I'm finished here anyway."

"If you are, then I must be, too." A hint of laughter ran through his words. "Should we put them back in their stalls now, or what?"

Right. She couldn't simply abandon him when he didn't know the routine.

Emmett came around the corner of the barn. "You two all done?"

"I think for now we are," Rafe said.

"I'll take those two and turn 'em loose in the pasture for you. Did you have fun?"

"Sure did." Rafe untied Destiny and led him over toward Meg. "I wouldn't mind a repeat tomorrow."

"There, see?" Emmett clapped him on the shoulder. "I knew you'd take to it." He glanced at Meg. "You look a little flushed, girl."

Meg swallowed. "I'm fine."

Rafe handed Destiny's lead rope to Emmett. "You do look flushed, Meg." He glanced over at Emmett. "She was just mentioning that she thought it was quite warm out there."

"Honestly, I'm fine." Or she would be, once she got away from the major heat source in the black Stetson.

"Even so, you'd better head on up to the house for a cool drink." Emmett gave her a fatherly smile. "Don't want anyone falling by the wayside before the big day."

"That's for sure." Rafe slung a casual arm over her shoulders. "Come on, you. Let's get you cooled off." He gave her a little push toward the house before letting his arm slide free.

She tingled everywhere he'd touched her. "It's your fault, you know," she murmured.

"Yes, but you started it," he said in a cheerful tone. "And for your information, I'm a writhing mass of frustration inside."

"I don't believe you. Emmett didn't mention that you looked flushed."

"My reaction takes place a little lower. I've been struggling to keep my pride and joy under control so I can walk."

"Well, for your information, I have a reaction going on a little lower, too."

"Good. I'll take full responsibility for your damp panties if you'll take full responsibility for my pinched penis."

She nearly choked on a laugh.

"You okay?"

She nodded and cleared her throat. "Listen, we need to stop this or we'll never make it through the day."

"You're not having fun?"

"I didn't say that, but what if I snap and drag you upstairs in broad daylight?"

"That would give everyone something to talk about

besides the problem of my mother. For all you know, we'd be doing them a favor by creating a diversion."

She looked over at him and grinned. "Interesting idea, but if it's all the same to you, I'd rather not be the main topic of conversation around the ranch."

"I'm just sayin'. So if you happen to lose control and haul me upstairs, it wouldn't be all bad."

"I'll keep that in mind."

"But if you're not feeling inclined to do that right this minute, I think I'll turn on my cell phone."

She gave a guilty start. "Good grief, by all means. I hope you weren't waiting for my permission."

"Well, no. It's the damnedest thing. When I'm with you, I forget all about work." He pulled his phone out of his pocket. "I can't say that happens very often."

"I'll take that as a compliment."

"I guess it is, but that also means you could become a liability." He powered up the phone.

Her happiness ebbed a bit. "That doesn't sound nearly as nice."

"Don't worry." He scrolled through his messages. "I won't let that happen."

Happiness gave way to irritation. "I wasn't worried. I was insulted. What do you mean, I could become a *liability?* You make me sound like a bad investment."

He frowned and glanced over at her. "Sorry. I didn't catch all that."

"Never mind." Nothing like a guy mesmerized by the information coming through his iPhone to kill the mood. She started up the porch steps, unwilling to compete with technology for his attention.

"Meg, wait." He caught her arm. "You're upset. What's the matter?"

She turned. A step above him, they were eye to eye, nose to nose. Also mouth to mouth, but she wasn't in a kissing mood. "You said I could become a liability. I don't appreciate being told that."

He winced. "Yeah, that was a bonehead thing to say. I didn't mean it like it sounded."

"How did you mean it, then?"

"It's the way financial types talk. Everything's viewed in terms of assets and liabilities. If something boosts the bottom line, it's an asset. If it doesn't, then—"

"Spare me the economic lecture, Rafe. I know about assets and liabilities. I want to know why you're so ready to dump me into the second category."

"Because you're so vibrant and sexy that when I'm with you, I forget everything else. That's good, and I really like the way I feel when I'm with you, but it's also a little scary."

She blinked. He'd actually admitted that he was afraid? That was progress. He must be venturing outside his comfort zone for him to say something like that.

"The thing is, if I'm going to do my job, I can't afford to zone out on a regular basis. I only meant that if I allowed myself to focus on you all the time, I'd be in danger of letting my work suffer."

Time to calm his fears. "In what world would I monopolize your time? Or allow you to monopolize mine? This week is an aberration for both of us. Normally I'm working, too, plus I have friends and family and plenty of my own interests. Furthermore, I respect your time and your work. I would *never* suck up chunks of your life to the point I'd become a *liability*."

He looked stunned. "No, of course you wouldn't. If I'd taken time to think, I would have realized that. It *was* an insulting thing to say, and you have a right to be angry. I'm sorry."

He looked so miserable that the anger leaked right out of her. In truth, he had paid her a huge compliment. Apparently not much came between Rafe and his precious work.

But she had, for one golden morning. Although she'd meant what she'd said about not sucking up chunks of his life, she wouldn't mind freeing him from his shackles once in a while. If not her, then who?

"It's okay." She smiled at him. "Go ahead and check your stock prices and whatever else you need to do. I'm going to take a quick shower before lunch." She started to leave.

"Wait. The message I was reading was from Wyatt. He and Olivia have a break between appointments, and they wanted to know if we'd meet them for lunch at the Spirits and Spurs. He said it might be the only time the four of us could get together before things get crazy."

"Sure. I'd love that."

"Good." He seemed immensely relieved that she wasn't upset with him anymore. "I'll text him that we'll be there in…" He glanced up. "How soon?"

"Thirty minutes."

"Great. I'll tell him."

"That should give you a little time to check in at work."

He grimaced and shook his head. "I have a feeling I'm going to regret that liability remark for a long time."

"Nah." She touched his hand. "You can make me forget everything else, too, including bonehead remarks." Leaving him to mull that over, she ran up the steps and into the house.

Rafe got ready quickly while ignoring the fact that Meg was right down the hall in the shower. Now was not the time for fun and games. They were due in town, and besides, he felt a little off balance after their last exchange. So he freshened up and waited for her at the bottom of the winding staircase that connected the first and second floors.

While he waited, he tapped the borrowed Stetson against his thigh as he replayed their flare-up. The conclusion was obvious—he'd been an ass and she'd called him on it.

Fortunately she seemed willing to forgive him and let the subject drop. Fine with him. They had so little time to enjoy each other that he didn't want to waste any of it on arguments.

No question that he was in uncharted territory with Meg. After one morning with her, he realized how superficial his relationships with women had been up to this point. She was the first one to get under his skin, and in trying to explain that, he'd almost blown his chance to be with her.

She was so different from the women he usually dated. He'd gravitated toward a cool exterior, someone who didn't get too excited about anything, someone who skimmed over the top of life and avoided emotional depths. Pleasant women. Undemanding women.

He hadn't demanded anything of them, either. No wonder he hadn't considered marrying any of them. He'd never bothered to get to know who they were, and vice versa.

Two days ago that kind of life had made perfect sense. Now he wondered what it said about him that he'd been satisfied with such tepid encounters. He'd never thought of himself as a coward, and yet...

"Let's go!" She came bouncing down the stairs in a crisp white blouse tucked into a fresh pair of jeans. Instead of boots, she wore sneakers with daisies all over them. She'd also ditched the Western hat in favor of sunglasses perched on top of her head, and she had a denim purse slung over her shoulder.

Apparently she liked to come at life from many angles. He'd met the cowgirl and the seductress. This afternoon she was the girl next door. Her mop of red curls and sunny smile filled his heart with joy. "You look terrific."

"Thanks." She joined him at the bottom of the stairs and gave him a once-over. "So do you. How many spare outfits did Sarah have?"

"Only two." He walked to the door and opened it for her. "After this I'm back to my slacks and dress shirts."

"Noo."

He laughed at her exaggerated distress. "If it makes you that unhappy, I could find out where the washer and dryer are in this place."

"You could." She glanced over her shoulder at him as she walked out the door. "Or we could go shopping."

Shopping for his clothes sounded a little too domestic and intimate. "Nah, I'll just wash what I have." Closing the door, he followed her down the porch steps.

"But don't you need to buy some dressy Western wear for the wedding?"

"So Wyatt said." He led the way toward the Lexus that was still parked in the drive. Maybe he ought to move it when they came back. "At some point I'll go to Jackson and pick up what he suggested."

"That makes sense." Some of the cheer had left her voice. "Didn't mean to push."

He blew out a breath as he opened the passenger door for her. "You weren't pushing, Meg." He might have to officially admit that he *was* a coward, scared to death of letting someone get too close. "What would you say if I told you I've never shopped for clothes with a woman I'm dating?"

She glanced up at him as she slid onto the leather seat. "I'd say you're a very private man. I'll keep that in mind."

In that instant he could see the wall going up between them, a very familiar and comfortable wall for him. He didn't think it would prevent them from having sex and enjoying some good times this week. But it would stop him from getting to know Meg on a deeper level, because if he held back, so would she.

As he closed the door and rounded the car to the driver's side, he realized that this was how he reacted with every woman. They'd reach a point where he would have to make a choice to be open or build a wall. He'd always chosen the wall.

What if he made a different choice this time? What if he used this week to find out if he could have a relationship that didn't involve a wall? If he ever planned to risk it, now seemed like a good time, and Meg seemed like the right woman, open, flexible, giving.

Climbing behind the wheel, he started the car, turned on the air and pulled out of the gravel driveway. "I think it's possible for a man to be too private," he said.

"Oh?" Caution echoed in that single syllable.

He hated hearing that note of hesitation and knew he'd put it there. "If you're offering to go with me to

Jackson this afternoon, I'd be honored to have you. I think it'll be boring as hell, but I—"

"Boring? No way!" The smile was back in her voice. "I *love* helping a gorgeous guy pick out clothes. I have all the fun, and you spend all the money. What could be better than that?"

He glanced over at her, and her face was alight with enthusiasm at the prospect. To think he'd almost deprived her—no, almost deprived *himself*—of the experience. And he wouldn't soon forget that she'd labeled him gorgeous. "I'm sorry I didn't take you up on the suggestion right away. I just—"

"Hey, it's not the way you usually operate. I get that. Knowing I'll be the first woman you've ever taken clothes shopping makes me feel special. I'll do my best not to be annoying."

"I can't imagine you being annoying."

"Trust me, I can be. Now that I know how good you look in this Western stuff, I'll be trying to get you to load up on it."

"And then what?" Rafe winced as the Lexus took a beating on the rutted road leading to the highway. "I can guarantee I won't be dressing like a cowboy in San Francisco."

"Are you sure you couldn't find times to wear jeans and boots? Not every guy wears jeans like you do."

"What, they put them on backward?"

"You know what I mean. You have a great butt, Rafe. You should show it off more."

That made him grin. "I'm not sure that's a good idea in San Francisco."

"Okay, maybe not," she said with a laugh. "Anyway, you'll be in possession of the credit card, so you can rein me in anytime. I don't think it would hurt to have a few extra outfits, though, now that Wyatt's moved here."

"So these would be my Wyoming vacation clothes." He stepped on the brake pedal as they came to the two-lane highway leading into the small town of Shoshone. After glancing both ways, he pulled out.

"Exactly," she said. "You want to fit in when you're here, and now that you're a horseback rider, you really need the right clothes."

"I'm not sure I can call myself a horseback rider yet."

"Sure you can. You were awesome for your first time. After a few more outings, you'll be— Rafe, look out!"

"Shit!" A red pickup was in their lane, coming straight at them.

7

M EG SCREAMED AND COVERED her face with both hands.
Not again. Please, not again! She braced for the impact, the sound of grinding metal and breaking glass,
followed by pain, incredible pain.

The car jerked violently, throwing her against her
seat belt. Every muscle in her body tensed, and then…
nothing. Gradually she became aware of Rafe beside
her, gasping for air.

"It's okay." He drew a shaky breath and his arm came
around her shoulders. "We're okay, Meg."

She dared to take her hands away and open her eyes.
The car was tilted to the right, off the road, and the engine was still running. She felt light-headed and did her
best to breathe, even though she felt as if a giant hand
squeezed her chest.

Someone rapped on Rafe's window. She watched in
silence as Rafe powered it down to reveal a teenager's
agonized stare.

"God, I'm sorry! Are you okay? Is anybody hurt? I
have a cell phone. I can call someone. Jesus. I'm so sorry."

Rafe heaved a sigh and shut off the motor. "I think

we're all right." He turned to look at Meg. "Meg? You okay?"

She nodded, unable to speak.

"I don't know what happened!" The kid seemed semihysterical. "When I checked before, the road was deserted, but then, suddenly, there you were! Thank God you have good reflexes, man. Listen, do you need a tow? I have rope. I can get you outta there."

"That might be a good idea." Rafe gave Meg's shoulder a quick squeeze. "Hang on. I'll supervise getting us hitched up to his truck, and then I'll be right back."

"My girlfriend is directing traffic so we won't get run over doing this. Man, I am so sorry."

"Things happen." Rafe unsnapped his seat belt and opened his door. The kid held it while he levered himself out. Once he was standing, he leaned down to give Meg a reassuring smile. "You might want to give Olivia a call and tell her we're running late."

Meg nodded again, although she couldn't call. She didn't want to admit that she'd tightened every muscle for fear that if she relaxed a single one, she'd start shaking uncontrollably. After three years, she'd imagined herself over the shock, but obviously she wasn't.

To be fair, she hadn't been tested until now. A couple of near-misses in a parking lot and having a driver stop suddenly in front of her—those minor close calls didn't count. They'd been nothing like this. She'd been convinced they would die.

Rafe and the kid, who wore a straw cowboy hat and looked no older than eighteen, worked together to attach a rope to the front of the car and the back of the pickup. Meg watched them and tried to keep herself together.

She longed to crawl into bed and curl up in a ball, but that wasn't an option.

Rafe opened the door and eased back inside the car. Then he started it up. "Once we're on the road again I'll be able to tell if there's any damage. The kid's insured, so no worries there." He looked over at Meg. "Were you able to get in touch with Olivia?"

"Not yet."

"She's probably turned off her phone. Did you leave a message? Whoops, here we go." He gripped the wheel as the rope tightened and the car gradually edged up the small embankment and back on the road. Rafe set the emergency brake and got out of the car again.

While Meg watched Rafe and the teenager disconnect the rope, exchange information and shake hands, she began to quiver. Apparently the shakes were going to take over, whether she wanted them to or not. Her teeth began to chatter.

When Rafe came back, he put the car in gear without looking at her and started down the road. "That's that. Or at least, I hope it is. I'll know in a few minutes if we have an alignment problem. Maybe not, but wow. Too close for comfort, huh?" He reached over and took her hand.

Once he touched her, he glanced sharply in her direction. "Meg? Good God, you're not okay, are you?"

"N-not r-really."

"There's a dirt road up ahead. I'll turn off there." He kept giving her worried looks as he approached the road, drove down it and shut off the engine. "What is it? Whiplash? Should I take you to a hospital? Hell, I don't even know where the nearest one is. Screw that. I'll call 9-1-1." He took his phone off the dash.

"No!"

He paused, his finger hovering over the phone. "Meg, you're scaring me. If something's wrong, then I want to get help."

"I j-just need s-somebody to hold m-me."

He was out of the car in a flash and came immediately around to her side. Opening her door, he reached in and unfastened her seat belt, then scooped her up and deposited her in the backseat. He climbed in after her, tossed his hat into the front and pulled her onto his lap.

"Y-you're so w-warm."

"And you're cold as ice." He held her tight. "And shaking like a leaf. I should have realized it sooner."

She clung to him and burrowed against his solid chest. She couldn't seem to get close enough.

"You're okay." He stroked her back and kissed her hair. "You're safe, Meg."

Slowly her tremors subsided, and once they had, she took a shaky breath. "Better."

"Good." He continued to stroke her back. "Take your time. We're in no rush."

"But Livy and Wyatt…"

"I'll call them in a little while, just so they won't worry."

"The thing is…three years ago…I was in…a very bad accident."

Rafe groaned. "No wonder you're a mess." He rocked her gently. "Poor Meg."

"No, *lucky* Meg. I should have died. But I didn't, which everyone said was a miracle."

His arms tightened around her. "That's scary."

"This was the first close call I've had since then. I lost it. Sorry."

"Don't be. You had a perfectly logical reaction. I wish it hadn't happened, but life's unpredictable."

"Exactly. But I didn't always understand that. The accident changed me." Resting her cheek against his chest, she listened to his steady heartbeat and thought how precious that sound was.

"I can imagine it would."

"I'd always been a fairly positive person, but when I realized how easily life can be snuffed out, I vowed to make the most of still being alive, against all odds."

"Which explains why you're so ready to try new things."

"You don't know the half of it. I have a list."

"A bucket list?"

"Sort of, but I'd rather think of it as my celebration-of-life list."

He kissed the top of her head. "Would you show it to me sometime?"

"Sure. But it's not a set list. It's always changing. Some things drop off after I've done them, and other things are added as I think of them."

"I see."

Shifting position, she gazed up at him. "For instance, you're on it now."

He looked into her eyes and smiled. "And exactly how am I on it?"

Her pulse quickened. "I'll bet you can guess."

"I sure hope so. Will I get checked off tonight?"

"I suppose that's possible." She reached up and traced his mouth with her finger. "But I have a feeling once won't be enough."

"I have the same feeling." Leaning down, he captured her lips in a slow, sensuous kiss.

She kissed him back, enthusiasm mingled with gratitude that they'd survived. The kiss quickly heated up and he'd started unbuttoning her blouse when both of their cell phones belted out simultaneous ring tones.

He lifted his head, his gaze hot. "Later."

"It's a date." She climbed off his lap and they both reached into the front seat for their phones so they could assure the bride and groom that all was well.

Rafe wasn't sure what haunted him more—the harrowing experience on the road today or the knowledge that Meg had nearly died in an accident three years ago. As he pulled into the dirt parking lot next to the Spirits and Spurs, he admitted that Meg's decision to fully embrace life made a lot of sense.

As he switched off the engine, she unbuckled her seat belt and reached for her door.

"Will you let me help you out?" he asked.

She paused and turned to him. "I'm really fine. You don't have to baby me."

"That's not why I want to do it. I think of it as a gesture of…caring. I realize you're capable of getting out of a car by yourself, but then I lose the chance to be gallant."

She smiled. "You were very gallant when I went through that meltdown."

"I hope so. I never gave it much thought before, but gallantry appeals to me. Some women object to it on the grounds that I'm not treating them like an equal."

She took her hand off the door. "I won't. I'm secure in my equality."

"Good to know." He couldn't help chuckling. She was such a fascinating combination of spunkiness and vulnerability.

"The longer I'm around you, Rafe, the more I think you really are a cowboy underneath that sophisticated exterior."

"City boys can be gallant, too, you know."

"I'm sure, but it seems to go with the life out here, somehow. To me, cowboys are the modern equivalent of knights in armor, and when I think of gallantry, I think of knights."

"In that case, I'll be as much of a cowboy this week as I can manage, given my limitations." He climbed out of the car and walked around to her side feeling happy to be alive. Meg helped him keep his priorities straight.

When they walked into the Spirits and Spurs he had the unwelcome thought that his mother would hate it there. His father might, too. It was old, and the tables were scarred from years of hard use. The overriding smell indicated that beer was more popular than any other beverage.

A few days ago, Rafe probably would have turned up his nose at the idea of having lunch in a cowboy beer joint. Yet now he could hardly wait to slide into a booth and order up a pitcher and some eats. It suddenly seemed like the most fun he could have, short of taking Meg to bed. And he looked forward to enjoying that tonight.

The place was full of lunch patrons enjoying exactly the kind of meal Rafe had in mind—a juicy burger and a big pile of fries. His parents would roll their eyes, but they weren't here, and he was enjoying a sense of liberation. Wyatt and Olivia waved from a booth across the room, and he put his hand in the small of Meg's back and guided her over to them.

Olivia jumped up and gave Meg a hug. "How awful for you, sweetie! I hate that you went through that."

Wyatt slid out of the booth and held his hand out to his brother. "Thanks for getting here safe and sound, bro. I wonder if we need to haul that kid into traffic court. He shouldn't have—"

"It was a rookie mistake," Rafe said. "He looked terrified, and I doubt he'll try anything like that again without checking and double-checking. I think he'll punish himself enough reliving that moment when we almost crashed."

Olivia shuddered and glanced at Meg. "I can only imagine what went through your mind."

"You probably can. You were there to get me past the trauma three years ago."

"I was." She looked over at Rafe. "Did she tell you she had a near-fatal accident?"

"Yeah." And Rafe was so grateful that she had told him. If their positions had been reversed, he wondered if he would have been that willing to share. He had much to learn from Meg.

Wyatt studied his brother and his gray eyes twinkled. "Nice duds there, Rafe. Did Sarah fix you up?"

"As a matter of fact, she did."

"Well done." Wyatt gestured to the table. "As you can see, Olivia and I started on a pitcher, but let's get another one and have some food. What sounds good?" Then he hesitated. "Or maybe we should rustle up a bottle of wine. I'm sure they have—"

"Beer's fine," Rafe said. "In fact, beer and a burger would be perfect for me, but I can't speak for Meg."

Wyatt looked surprised, but he didn't make a comment.

"I'd be very happy with a burger and a beer," Meg said. "At this point, I could use some comfort food."

"Coming up." Wyatt signaled a waitress and gestured for Rafe and Meg to have a seat. After the waitress took their order, he glanced across the table at his brother. "How was the ride this morning?"

"Good." Rafe nodded. "It was good."

"Rafe was amazing," Meg said. "He picked up on the basics in no time. I think we have a cowboy on our hands."

"Really?" Wyatt raised both eyebrows. "I never would have figured that."

"Meg's exaggerating. I had beginner's luck. Besides, they put me up on Destiny, the old man of the barn. I couldn't go wrong."

Olivia laughed. "I've heard tales of that horse from when Jack was teaching Josie to ride a couple of years ago. Isn't Destiny the one who likes to head on home if his rider gets off and doesn't tie him up good?"

"That's the one." Meg grimaced. "I tied Destiny to my horse, and before we realized it, Spilled Milk was ready to lay into Destiny because he was trying to drag her away from her station."

Wyatt looked amused as he glanced from Meg to Rafe. "So, brother-of-mine, you didn't notice that the horses were getting snippy with each other?"

Rafe gave Wyatt the evil eye. "We were admiring the spectacular scenery. It's easy to get caught up in the view when you're in this part of the country."

"So it is." Wyatt picked up his mug of beer and took a sip while unsuccessfully hiding a grin.

"Are the caterers all set for Saturday?" Meg asked.

Rafe could recognize a change of subject when he heard one, and he followed her lead. "Yeah, how's everything going? As the best man I need to know these things."

"The caterers are all set," Olivia said. "We'll double-check on the flower delivery after lunch to make sure what we ordered will actually be here."

"I feel as if I should be doing more," Rafe said. "Are you sure you don't want me to organize a bachelor party?"

Wyatt shook his head. "Olivia and I would ten times rather have a party here for everyone Thursday night. This tradition of separating the men and women doesn't work for us."

"So I might as well cancel the stripper." Rafe sighed as if bitterly disappointed.

"Maybe not." Olivia shared a glance with Meg. "Did you hire a man or a woman?"

"He didn't hire either one," Wyatt said, "because I told him not to." He paused. "You didn't, right?"

"No, I followed your instructions, but from the way the female contingent is looking at me, maybe we need to rethink this. Ladies, do you want a male stripper at the party Thursday night?"

Olivia leaned forward. "Could we have a guy wearing tight jeans and chaps?"

"And shirtless, but with a leather vest," Meg added. "And spurs on his boots. I want him to jingle when he walks."

"Yes!" Olivia and Meg exchanged high fives across the table.

"Ooo, and leather gloves with fringe, right, Livy?"

"You have such good taste, Meg. You can create my fantasy cowboy any day."

Wyatt groaned. "Pay no attention to them, Rafe. They have a warped idea of what looks good on a man."

"It's what looks good coming *off* a man that's important," Meg said.

"Keep talking." Rafe pulled a napkin out of the dispenser. "If someone can loan me a pen, I'll make some notes so I get this right."

Meg turned to him. "For Thursday night?"

He winked at her. "That, too."

8

ALL THE KIDDING AROUND at lunch helped Meg relax and forget about the incident on the road into town, but once she and Rafe were headed for Jackson on another two-lane road, she tensed up again. Not good. This week would involve lots of time riding in cars and trucks.

"A leather vest with no shirt, huh?" Rafe glanced over at her. "That's what it takes?"

"It's a start." She tried her best to sound upbeat and teasing. Maybe Rafe wouldn't notice that she wasn't quite into it.

"I don't know about the chaps, though. That might be overkill."

"Possibly so." She'd conquer this case of nerves. She had to.

His response was a couple of beats late, and he'd switched topics on her. "I'm really curious about this list of yours. Can you tell me more about what you've already done?"

That brief hesitation and change in topic told her he'd guessed that she was nervous about being back on the road. Instead of asking her about it, he'd decided to subtly remind her of moments she'd been strong and brave. That kind of empathy didn't come along every day.

"I tried hang gliding last year when I was in San Diego for a traffic control conference."

"Did you like it?"

"You bet. My job takes up too much time, so I haven't gone back to it. If I change jobs and move here, I'm looking for a less time-consuming position so I can build in breaks for things like that."

"You might have to take a pay cut."

"That's okay. I don't need a lot of money." She watched with some apprehension as they came up behind a slow-moving semi. No doubt Rafe would want to get around the truck. Well, she'd just take a deep breath and keep calm.

"I've always wanted to try hang gliding. There's this guy named Hutchinson out of San Francisco who makes amazing videos of sports like that. Have you seen any of them?"

"I have, as a matter of fact. Did you know he was born in Shoshone and his dad runs the feed store there?"

"Huh. Small world."

"He's good friends with Jack Chance, and I'm pretty sure he'll be at the wedding. If so, you can meet him."

"I'd like that." He made no move to pass the truck. "So what else have you done?"

"Rafe, you don't have to poke along behind this truck. I'll be fine if you want to pass."

"We're in no rush."

"No, but we're doing ten miles under the speed limit. The truck's put on his left-turn signal twice to let you know you can go around."

"You're sure?"

"Yep."

He let out a breath. "Thank God." Easing out to check traffic, he tromped on the gas and the powerful car zoomed around the eighteen-wheeler and back over to the right side of the road. "I could tell you were still a little freaked out, so I didn't want to make it worse."

"I know, and I appreciate that." She gazed at him. Besides being the hunkiest chauffeur she'd ever had, he also looked relaxed and confident behind the wheel. The last of her tension drained away. "But I'm fine now."

"I believe you." He gave her a smile before returning his attention to the road. "I can hear it in your voice."

"You were smart to get me talking about my list."

He shrugged. "I just hated to think of you white-knuckling it all the way to Jackson. It's not your style."

Warmth flooded through her. "That might be the nicest thing you've said to me. It's *not* my style, which is why I hated falling apart like that. But you've been great about it. No wonder clients trust you with all their money."

"And that might be the nicest thing you've said to me."

"I'm worried about you, though, Rafe."

His eyebrows lifted. "Me? Why?"

"I have a bad feeling you're all work and no play."

"No, I'm not. I go out to dinner. I catch a movie now and then."

"That's all fine, but I mean something exciting to get your blood pumping."

His smile was incredibly sexy. "I didn't think it was appropriate to mention *that* kind of excitement, considering the plans you and I have tonight."

"Oh, for heaven's sake. I didn't mean sex. I meant like taking a sailboat out on San Francisco Bay."

"I've done that."

"When?"

"Um, maybe ten years ago. My friend who had a boat sold it." He passed another slow-moving truck. "Would you like to go sailing on the bay?"

"Is that an invitation?"

"Absolutely. If you ever come to San Francisco, I'll take you sailing. Give me some advance warning, and I'll brush up my skills. You'd love it."

And so would he, she thought. The next part wasn't easy to say, but she made herself say it. "You don't have to wait for me to come to San Francisco. I'll bet there are plenty of women who would be thrilled if you took them sailing."

"I'd rather wait for you."

"Why on earth would you wait? It might be a year or two before I show up. And I can tell you want to do it."

"With you, yeah, but not with some random woman who might or might not get a kick out of going. I have no doubt that you would eat it up with a spoon, and we'd have a great time."

He was so cautious and guarded. She didn't know all the reasons why, but she could guess from things Olivia had said. Rafe and Wyatt's self-absorbed mother hadn't given them much attention and their workaholic father hadn't, either. Rafe seemed to have modeled himself after his dad, maybe hoping for approval from at least one parent.

She decided not to push the issue anymore. Obviously work and a familiar routine had been his shield for many years. If it lacked exhilarating highs, at least it didn't have devastating lows, either.

But she wouldn't give up on him. Their successful horseback ride told her that he still had the capacity to cut loose, and his kiss told her that a passionate man lurked under his careful exterior. Tonight she'd find out exactly how passionate he could be, and she could hardly wait.

RAFE TURNED THE CONVERSATION back to Meg's list, and she allowed him to do that. He found out about her hike through the Alps, and her future plan to walk the Great Wall someday soon. Her list ranged from spending an entire day at the Louvre in Paris to bungee jumping in Queenstown, New Zealand.

He was relieved that she'd seemed to give up on her campaign to inject some excitement into his San Francisco life. She might have a demanding job with the City of Pittsburgh, but he doubted she could imagine the pressures he faced every day, knowing the financial effect his recommendations could have on his wealthy clients. Planning a sailing date with someone he didn't know well would only add to his stress.

Still, as he listened to her describe the things she'd done and those she planned to do, he got caught up in her excitement. He wouldn't mind tagging along on some of those trips. Finding the time would be a challenge, but her enthusiasm was infectious.

He decided not to mention his interest, though. Such plans were more of a pipe dream than a reality for him. If she thought he wanted to go, she might start counting on it, and he couldn't promise that.

They finally arrived in Jackson, a town crowded

with cars bearing out-of-state plates. He had to circle the square twice before a parking spot opened up. But when it did, he pulled in right in front of the store he was headed for. Wyatt had told him which one would carry clothes suited to the wedding plus anything else he decided to buy for his own use.

Although he'd balked at taking Meg with him at first, now he was glad she'd suggested coming along. What would have been a boring trip to buy clothes he didn't actually want could turn into a great afternoon. Meg had a gift for making everything seem special.

She waited for him to help her out of the car, but once she was out, she was in bouncy tour-guide mode. "In that far corner of the square is the vintage clothing shop where Olivia and I found our dresses for the wedding. Next to it is Silver Reflections, the jewelry shop where I bought the earrings I wore last night."

"I liked those. I wonder if you need another pair." The idea of buying her jewelry was much more appealing than shopping for his clothes.

"Not really. I don't dress up that much." She pointed across the square. "Over there in the middle of the block is the gallery that carries Dominique's photography. If we have time after buying your stuff, we should go over."

"She's Nick's wife, right?" He hoped by the day of the wedding he'd have all the vitals of this family down.

"Right. It was pictures of Nick in cowboy mode that launched her career in Jackson Hole." Meg looked him up and down. "Has Dominique seen you in those clothes yet?"

"If she's the tall one with short brown hair..."

"That's her."

"Then, no. In the kitchen this morning I met the red-head and her little girl."

"That's Morgan, Gabe Chance's wife, and little S.B., aka Sarah Bianca. Anyway, I'll bet Dominique would love to get some shots of you in full garb. She's been after Jack to do it, and he won't, but you look so much like him, she might pounce on you instead."

Rafe shook his head. "She'll have to keep hounding Jack. I feel like enough of a fraud wearing this stuff without having pictures of me on display somewhere."

"I doubt Dominique will take that as a valid excuse, but you can try." She turned back toward the Western clothing store. "Ready to put a dent in your credit card?"

"I don't mind that part. But let's make this as quick as possible. Even if you don't get dressed up much, I'd like to check out the jewelry shop."

She smiled at him. "You don't have to buy me jewelry, Rafe."

"I know. But I'd like to."

"So I'll think of you when I wear it?"

He blinked at the accuracy of her statement. That was exactly what he wanted, although he hadn't realized it until she'd said so. He didn't want to fade out of her memory at the end of the week.

"I'll think of you whether you buy me jewelry or not," she said softly. "So save your money for other things, like a ticket back to Jackson Hole at Christmas."

"I can afford both."

She gazed at him and finally her green eyes began to twinkle with laughter. "So be it. If you want to throw your money around on jewelry for me, I'd be a fool to turn it down."

"I'm glad you've seen the light. Maybe we should do that first."

"No." She laced her fingers through his and tugged. "Come on, Rafe. Take your medicine like a man."

"All right." He sighed and walked with her toward the store. "But I want to start with the leather vests."

She paused and glanced at him. "Are you serious?"

"Isn't that what you said turned you on?"

"Yes, but I didn't think you'd actually be willing to buy one."

"Hey, now that you've confessed one of your fantasies, I might as well work it."

She grinned. "I like your attitude. You'll have to try it on without a shirt so I can tell if it's the right look. Will you do that?"

"*No.* For God's sake, Meg. I'll buy the vest, but I'm not parading around in the store wearing a vest and no shirt underneath. I'll look like an idiot."

"Then if you won't come out of the dressing room wearing the vest, I'll have to come in."

He stared at her. "I don't think so."

"If I did, I could check something else off my list."

"What?"

"Making out with a cute guy in a dressing room." Her cheeks were pink with excitement. "It's number fourteen."

He recognized a challenge when he heard one. She was daring him to go along with her crazy idea. And the more he thought about it, the more turned on he was. Maybe this shopping trip wouldn't be so boring, after all.

Squeezing her hand, he reached for the door. "First we have to find out if they have any vests that you like."

"If they don't, maybe you'd model some chaps without your—"

"That's where I draw the line, toots."

She laughed as they walked into a store that he instantly recognized as exclusive. Exclusive stores often had full doors on the dressing rooms. He began to anticipate getting Meg alone in one of them.

Glancing around, he noticed that the place catered to manly men. One wall held nothing but boots and belts, and the scent of oiled leather permeated the store. Jeans and shirts were neatly folded on planks supported by oak barrels. Any vacant wall space had been filled with coiled ropes, spurs and branding irons.

Rafe counted about six people shopping and at least two sales ladies. One of them, a middle-aged woman wearing a sparkly Western shirt and red jeans beamed as she walked in their direction. "May I help you?"

"I need something for a wedding at the Last Chance this weekend," Rafe said. "I'm the best man."

"Yes, of course. That would be the Locke-Sedgewick wedding."

"That's right. Meg is going to help me pick out something."

"Perfect." The woman started toward the back of the store. "If you'll both follow me, I'll show you the jackets first."

"Thanks." He stroked his thumb over Meg's palm. "Oh, and by the way, do you happen to carry any leather vests?"

"We do, but a leather vest worn under your Western jacket will get quite warm this time of year. If you want the look of a vest, I suggest fabric."

Meg spoke up. "The leather vest is for...another time."

"Ah." The woman glanced over her shoulder at Meg. "So you're also interested in some articles that aren't specifically wedding-related."

Meg nodded. "We are. In fact, if you'll point me toward the leather vests, you and Rafe can discuss jackets."

"They're on the far left wall hanging below our display of hats."

"Be right back." Meg slipped her hand from his and with a saucy little wink went in search of vests.

Rafe watched her go. He didn't hear the saleswoman's question until she tapped him on the arm. He turned to her and felt heat rising up from his collar. "Sorry. You were saying?"

"What color jacket are you interested in?"

"The groom said I should look for something in dove-gray."

"Excellent choice. Let's see what we have in your size."

Rafe managed to pay attention long enough to give her his coat size and pretend interest as she handed him three different jackets on sturdy wooden hangers.

"And you'll need Western dress slacks to go with that. Those are over here." The woman started moving toward a different section of the store.

"Wait a sec. I don't want to lose Meg."

The saleswoman chuckled. "Oh, I'm sure she'll find you."

Of course she would, but he didn't want her to go hunting all over the store. That would waste time, and

he could hardly wait to find a way to slip into one of
the dressing rooms and…

"Waist and inseam?"

He focused on the saleswoman again and gave her
his measurements. Then he scanned the store, looking
for that bright mass of curls bobbing around somewhere
in the aisles. And there she was, coming toward him
with an armful of leather vests and a triumphant grin
that made him want to laugh out loud.

He'd never shop for clothes again without thinking of
her smug expression as she brought him the makings of
her cowboy fantasy. He hoped to hell he could live up
to the image she carried in that creative mind of hers.

9

Meg walked with Rafe over to the hallway that led to a row of dressing rooms, but she didn't want their ever-helpful sales lady to guess her intention. She piled the vests on top of the clothes Rafe already held in his arms. "Go ahead and try everything on," she said. "I'll be out here if you want to show me anything." Then she sat primly in one of the two leather wing chairs near the dressing rooms.

"I'll just put you in number three," the woman said. "My name is Clara. Let me know if you need any different sizes."

Rafe cast a quick glance at Meg. "Thanks so much, Clara. I'm sure something out of this pile will work." Then he walked into the dressing room and closed the door.

While her pulse danced a jig, Meg counted to sixty. Then, making sure nobody was watching, she walked quickly to Rafe's dressing room and turned the knob. He'd locked it.

Rapping softly, she lowered her voice. "It's me."

The door opened immediately and he pulled her inside. "Sorry. Habit." Then he crushed her against his chest and brought his mouth down on hers.

Rafe had the sort of kiss that demanded her full attention, and yet as she wrapped her arms around him, she realized that his were bare. And he was wearing one of the leather vests.

Although she couldn't see him, her roving hands provided enough tactile evidence to visualize her fantasy, and she moaned softly as she wiggled closer. The scent of leather and aroused male released a flood of happy hormones into her system.

He lifted his mouth from hers. "Is this what you had in mind?"

"Oh, yeah." She kissed his chin, moved down to the sexy hollow in his throat, and kept on going. Spreading the lapels of the vest aside, she licked her way to each flat nipple as she stroked his soft chest hair.

"Meg." His voice was strained. "Maybe you shouldn't do that."

"Yes, I definitely should. You're delicious." She used her tongue to trace a moist path to his navel and felt him shudder.

When she dropped to her knees and reached for his zipper, he closed his hand over hers. "I don't think—"

"Right. Don't think." Pushing his hand away, she drew the zipper down. Blood pounded in her ears. She'd never been so bold with a man in a public place. Then again, she'd never been so inspired to be bold.

He might have protested, but he was more than ready for her. When she dipped her hand inside the opening of his briefs, his erect cock surged forward. She took a moment to caress and admire the beauty of it.

If he really wanted to stop her, he could do it now.

But instead he trembled and thrust his fingers through her hair. She took him into her mouth.

He tasted of forbidden pleasures and untamed lust. Her heart raced as she measured the length of him with her lips and tongue. He was magnificent, and tonight he would be all hers.

This was only a short preview, and she couldn't take long or someone would suspect. Hollowing her cheeks, she applied pressure right where she knew it would accomplish the most good. His fingers tightened against her scalp, and he gasped once before his hot, salty essence filled her mouth.

Swallowing what he'd given her, she remained still for a moment as he fought to get his breathing under control. Then she slowly released him, tucked him back into his briefs, and zipped his fly. Then she rose, nibbling her way back up his body until she finally reached his lips.

He kissed her deeply before drawing back, his dark eyes smoldering and his voice husky. "That was amazing."

"Glad you enjoyed it."

A sharp rap sounded on the dressing room door. "Finding anything you like?" called the saleswoman.

Gazing down at Meg, Rafe smiled. "Sure am."

"Good! Let me know if you need anything."

"Thanks, but this should do it."

Meg leaned back to survey the vest, which had been her favorite of the ones she'd found. But she didn't dare speak until the saleswoman was gone.

"You chose well," she said at last, keeping her voice low. The leather was dark brown and supple, the design simple and slightly retro. It showed off Rafe's magnificent chest and sculpted arms to perfection.

"You don't want to see how the others look?"

She shook her head. "This one already has a very good association for me. I'd love to see it on you again."

"With that kind of reaction, I'll wear it any time you want. Sadly, now I have to pick out the boring stuff."

"I know. I'll be outside in the chair, ready to give my opinion."

He touched her cheek. "So, did we take care of number fourteen?"

"Fourteen *and* fifteen."

He laughed softly. "I really need to get a look at that list."

She fully intended to show it to him, but before she did, she might add a few things. Being with Rafe was expanding her horizons.

RAFE WASN'T SURE WHAT HE bought besides the vest. He was too blissed out from Meg's dressing-room treat to care what else went on his credit card. He suspected she'd used his mellow mood to talk him into more jeans and shirts than he would ever need.

Eventually they'd stashed the bags of clothes in the trunk of the Lexus and he put enough brain cells together to remember about the jewelry shop. "I still want to get you some earrings." Taking her hand, he started walking around the square.

"It's liable to cost you. Silver Reflections only sells Native American pieces and none of them are cheap. I splurged on those silver-and-turquoise ones."

"I feel in the mood to splurge."

"You may not realize it because you were sort of

catatonic back there in the Western-wear store, but you already splurged. You might want to pull out your sales slip and reconsider a trip to the jewelry store."

He shook his head. "That was all for me. I want something for you."

"The vest was for me."

He flashed back to the moment she'd slid to her knees in the dressing room. "Maybe so, but I made out like a bandit on that vest deal. I think we could have a long argument as to who benefited the most from it."

"Do you think the saleswoman had any idea what was going on in there?"

"If she did, she's too good a salesperson to let a little thing like oral sex in the dressing room interfere with writing up a big order."

"Aha!" She glanced up at him. "So you did realize that we ran up a sizable bill in there. I thought maybe you were oblivious."

"Oblivious to the type and amount of clothes." He smiled at her. "But finances are my game. I'm incapable of ignoring the bottom line, so believe me, I saw and registered the total."

"You could have objected."

"Nope. That was the best shopping trip of my life. If I end up giving half of those things to charity, I don't care. I don't have a list like yours, but if I did, I'd put getting a blow job in a dressing room right near the top."

"Woo-hoo!" Meg let go of his hand and threw her arms in the air. "Progress in the having-fun department!"

"Don't get cocky. This doesn't mean I plan to take some unidentified woman sailing on San Francisco Bay."

"About that."

"You can talk until you're blue in the face, Meg, but I'm not doing it. I now have a mental picture of taking you out there, and I'm sticking with that scenario. It's you or nobody."

"That suits me fine."

"It does?" He recaptured her hand. "I thought you were determined to get me out on a boat, with or without you."

"I suggested that because I didn't want to hold you back, but…it turns out I don't want you taking some other woman sailing."

"Oh?" He couldn't help feeling really great about that.

"I'm not proud of myself for saying so, Rafe. A true friend would want you to enjoy yourself, even if she couldn't be there."

"Correct me if I'm wrong, but I think we've gone a few steps past friendship. Not that we can't be friends, too, but what happened back in the dressing room adds another layer of meaning, don't you think?"

"It wouldn't have to. We could write it off as one of those thrilling little moments that is here and gone."

"Some people might be able to do that, those who skate along on the surface of their emotions." The way he'd been accustomed to doing until he'd met her. "You don't strike me as that kind of person."

"Well, I'm not, but on the other hand, we both agreed we're not looking for anything permanent."

He wondered if she was trying to convince him or her. "Right. No strings, no obligations. But the sailing date was your idea, so I'm reserving that experience for you and me. Does that work for you?"

She smiled up at him. "Perfectly. It's simple, really. Any activity we discuss doing together is reserved for us."

"Like me giving you skiing lessons this winter?"

"Precisely. And if you want a hang gliding buddy, I'm your girl."

His girl. The thought made his breath catch, but in a good way. He wondered if they were both kidding themselves about the future of this relationship. One of them might get invested, after all, and he had a funny feeling it could be him.

Yet if he knew she didn't want that, he could put on the brakes if he had to. Maybe everything would work out the way she envisioned and they'd meet at various times to sail, ski, hang glide and make love, all without a commitment of any kind.

It was an interesting concept and the only one that made sense considering his schedule. He'd have to juggle his work in order to find time for those activities, but he'd do it. The prospect of seeing Meg several times a year was worth crunching his other obligations.

Silver Reflections was a small shop, but dense with shiny stuff. Rafe hadn't been inside many jewelry stores, but he was used to cases of gems like diamonds, rubies and emeralds. This place didn't deal in precious stones.

Instead the cases included gold and silver decorated with turquoise, mostly, although there were other opaque stones in various colors. Rafe noticed a few ornate necklaces that seemed almost old-fashioned compared with the beautiful simplicity of others.

The shop was empty of customers when they walked in. The man behind the counter wore a Western shirt along with a bola tie containing a piece of turquoise as big as a hen's egg. He looked Native American, and his lined and weathered face could belong to a man of fifty or eighty. Rafe couldn't begin to guess his age.

He smiled. "Welcome."

"Thank you." Rafe expected more—an offer to sell them something, a suggestion about jewelry for the pretty lady—but the man said nothing else. Instead he simply watched them with polite interest.

Meg walked forward and held out her hand. "Hello, Samuel. I'm Meg. You probably don't remember, but I was in here a few days ago with my friend Olivia. We each bought earrings."

The man's face creased in a wider smile as he took her hand in both of his. "Now I remember who you are! Your friend is getting married."

"She is. On Saturday. This is Rafe Locke, the best man."

"Glad to meet you, Samuel." Rafe shook the man's hand and noticed he was also wearing a watch with a turquoise-studded band and a couple of elaborate turquoise rings.

"Samuel's a silversmith," Meg said. "He's made many of the pieces you see. Like that, for instance." She pointed to a dramatic necklace in the glass case.

"I noticed that when we came in." Rafe had never seen anything quite like it. A strip of polished silver about half an inch wide had been shaped to fit the back of a woman's neck and then spiral forward into an elegant coil that ended in a green stone the exact color of Meg's eyes. "I'd like to see what that looks like on."

Meg laughed and shook her head. "No, you wouldn't. It's way too expensive."

"I'm not saying we'll buy it, but I'm fascinated by the design. Samuel, would you mind if Meg tried it on?"

"Of course not." He unlocked the case and tenderly withdrew the necklace. "I remember you looked at this one last time, Meg, but you didn't ask me to show it to you." He took the tag off before handing the necklace to her.

"No point in that." Meg turned the necklace so it caught the light. "It's out of my price range. This is the sort of necklace Harrison Ford would buy for Calista."

Samuel nodded. "Harrison did look at it, as a matter of fact. But he couldn't decide, so it's still here, waiting for you."

"Not for me, but it's fun to think I'm trying on a necklace that Harrison Ford considered." Pulling aside the collar of her white shirt, she fit the molded silver end of the spiral around the back of her neck. "I love the idea that it doesn't need a fastener of any kind." She settled it against her breastbone, where it nestled as if made to rest there.

Rafe had known he'd buy the necklace for her the minute he'd seen it, but now that she had it on, he was even more convinced. "You need to undo one more button of your blouse to show it off."

"How scandalous." She winked at him and unfastened the button. "The silver feels cool on my skin."

"It'll warm up as you wear it," Samuel said. "Looks good on you. You're the right one for malachite."

"So that's malachite?" Rafe took a closer look at the stone, which had faint bands of black running through it. "I know nothing about these things, but I like it."

Samuel glanced at Meg. "When's your birthday?"

"Not for months, if you're thinking I need a birthday present, Samuel."

"No, I wasn't thinking that. I just wondered the day."

"November fifth. Why?"

Rafe blinked. His and Wyatt's birthday was November third.

Samuel looked pleased with himself. "*That's* why the necklace is so right for you. I had a feeling about you from the beginning. Malachite is your birthstone."

"I thought my birthstone was topaz."

"It can be, but so is malachite, and I personally think that's a more interesting choice."

"So do I," Rafe said. "We'll take it."

Meg's eyes widened. "We most certainly will *not* take it." She started to remove the necklace.

Rafe put a restraining hand over hers. "Meg, it's perfect on you." He glanced toward Samuel for backup. "Isn't it?"

"Yes." Samuel gazed at Meg. "I thought so the first time you came in the store, but then you left without it."

"For a very good reason. It's beyond my means."

"I understand that, but when I create a piece of jewelry, I always imagine who will wear it. You'll probably think I'm making this up, but it's the truth. When I worked on that necklace I imagined a woman with fiery hair and green eyes, a woman born in November who had a zest for life." He spread both hands. "And here you are."

"That's a lovely sentiment, but the necklace costs too much." She cast a pleading glance at Rafe. "Don't let yourself get carried away."

"You heard the man. He made the necklace for you." Rafe had listened to plenty of sales pitches in his life, and he recognized Samuel wasn't making one. The guy was an artist who wouldn't push his creations on those who didn't want them.

"We came in here for earrings," Meg said. "I'll accept a pair of earrings from you, Rafe, but this…"

Samuel pulled a small booklet out from under the counter. "Meg, what do you know about this stone?"

She turned back to the counter. "Only that it's pretty."

"It's more than pretty." He thumbed through the book. "Here we are—'malachite is a stone for the adventurous spirit, a risk-taker who yearns to live more fully and find unconditional love.'" He closed the book and gazed at her.

"Wow." She swallowed and placed her hand over the green stone. "That's…that's me."

Rafe felt a little shaky. That certainly described his brother, but he'd always thought he and Wyatt were polar opposites. Still, those words struck a deep chord in him, as well.

Maybe he wasn't so different from Wyatt, after all. He'd tried hard to be Wyatt's opposite, and…this was hard to admit, but he'd done it mostly to please his father. What had started out as the purchase of a beautiful piece of jewelry for Meg was turning out to be much more significant than he'd planned on.

"You notice I designed the necklace so it doesn't need a clasp," Samuel said.

Meg nodded.

"That wasn't just a random decision, or me trying to leap ahead of the pack with some clever innovation." His voice grew soft and slightly roughened with emotion. "I made it open-ended to signify freedom—

freedom to live and freedom to love. It needs to go to the right person."

"I don't think there's any doubt that Meg's the right person." Rafe pulled his wallet from his back pocket. "That's your necklace, Meg."

"But—"

"Furthermore, unless you object strongly, you should wear it out of the store." He took his credit card out and gave it to Samuel.

"Meg." Samuel looked at her. "Call me a crazy old man if you want, but I believe it's bad luck to refuse such a heartfelt gesture."

"Oh, I don't think you're crazy," Meg said. "But I'm not so sure about my friend Rafe, here."

Rafe wasn't convinced of his sanity, either. Buying a necklace, expensive or not, because the stone and the design had special significance wasn't typical of the Rafe Locke who'd arrived in Jackson Hole. The cost of the necklace hadn't bothered him at all and he'd have paid twice that to see Meg wearing the glorious spiral of silver.

But it wasn't the purchase of a high-end necklace making the ground shift beneath his feet. It was the growing suspicion that the woman wearing it had the power to change his life forever.

10

MEG KEPT TOUCHING THE necklace all the way back to the car. "I've never had anything this beautiful in my life," she said. "I don't know how I'll ever thank you."

"This would be the right time for me to make all kinds of lewd suggestions as to how you can thank me, but I won't, because I already have my thanks just looking at you wearing it."

"I wanted to scoff at his story about picturing someone like me as he made it, but..."

"I believe him. I'm sure he does that all the time, and when it works out, he's excited like he was today. I'm sure customers come in who aren't right for a piece he's made, but he has to sell it to them anyway. That must be a little frustrating."

"I feel like a princess wearing this."

He glanced over at her and smiled. "You'd be beautiful without it, but I have to admit I'm taken with how that bit of malachite directs me straight to your cleavage."

"And I thought you liked the malachite because it matches my eyes."

"That, too. Incidentally, Wyatt's and my birthday is two days before yours."

"Really? Then malachite is your birthstone, too."

"Guess so."

She thought about what Samuel had read out of the book he kept under the counter—*malachite is a stone for the adventurous spirit, a risk-taker who yearns to live more fully and find unconditional love.* "What did you think of that stuff Samuel read to us?"

"I'm still mulling it over."

She'd just bet he was. "Those things aren't always accurate." But she thought it described the person he could become, even if he wasn't there yet.

"I know." He looked over at her. "But it fits you to a T."

"I thought so, too. It was eerie. I was drawn to that necklace when I first saw it, but I figured it was the artistry of the design that pulled me in. It's so different. But I knew nothing about malachite or the properties he claims it has. Now I want to learn more."

"Your wish is my command." He pulled his iPhone out of his pocket as they reached the car. Leaning against the fender, he tapped on the screen. "I'll look it up on Google."

"I didn't think about it, but your phone hasn't rung once this afternoon."

"Kind of hard for it to ring when it's off."

"You turned it off? When?"

"When we got to the Spirits and Spurs. I didn't want anything interrupting our lunch, and then I didn't want to have it ringing while we drove up here."

"You didn't have to turn it off." She was amazed that he'd made that decision. "I wouldn't have minded."

"I would have minded. I wanted to talk to you, not to someone in San Francisco."

"Thank you." She admired how good he looked leaning against the fender in his jeans, boots, Western shirt and hat. A pickup truck would have suited the image better than the Lexus, but he seemed comfortable with the luxury car.

She didn't doubt that he made good money and the necklace hadn't been as damaging to his budget as it would have been to hers. That didn't mean she felt totally okay with his purchase. Yet Samuel had made a good point. When someone truly wanted to bestow a gift, it would be ungracious to refuse, even if she didn't believe it was bad luck as Samuel seemed to think.

Rafe glanced up from his phone. "Are you ready for the scoop on malachite?"

"I am." She touched the stone, which seemed warmer than it had when she put it on. It had probably soaked up some sun in addition to her body heat.

"Besides what Samuel told us, malachite is a stone of transformation."

"Is that so? Am I going to become a werewolf or something?"

He chuckled. "I don't think that's the kind of transformation they're talking about. They mention breaking outworn patterns and…oh, I like this part. It's supposed to release inhibitions." He glanced up from the screen and waggled his eyebrows at her.

Meg laughed. "So it will transform me into a wild woman?"

"I guess we'll see, won't we? And speaking of that, it's time to head back home via the drugstore."

"The drugstore? Why do we—" And then she remembered. "Oh, yes. The *drugstore*."

"And it's getting late. I'm sure Sarah expects us for dinner."

"She does. I had hoped we'd have time to stop at the gallery and take a look at Dominique's photographs, but we should probably skip that. I didn't expect to spend so much time in the jewelry store."

"I'm really glad we did, though." He shoved his phone back in his pocket and pulled out his car keys. "That necklace looks terrific on you."

"If malachite is your birthstone, shouldn't you be wearing it, too?"

"Sorry, but that necklace just doesn't go with my outfit." He opened the passenger door and ushered her in.

She rolled her eyes at him as she slid onto the leather seat. "I didn't mean the necklace, but something else, like a belt buckle with a piece of malachite on it."

"Now that *would* be a total waste of money. I might wear the jeans we bought on weekends, and possibly even the shirts sometimes, but there's no way in hell I'm walking around sporting a Western belt buckle like some urban cowboy."

"Okay, but don't be surprised if you end up being all inhibited because you resisted the power of the malachite."

Leaning down, he gave her a quick, hard kiss. "Something tells me if you lose your inhibitions, I'll give up on mine, too. We sort of proved that today in the dressing room. Now buckle up. We have to make tracks for the drugstore."

Meg had no idea where the nearest one was, but Rafe pulled up MapQuest on his phone and soon had them parked in front of what Rafe was now referring to as the "condom outlet."

"I'm sure people depend on this store for other things besides condoms," Meg said.

"I can't imagine what." He turned off the motor and unlatched his seat belt. "Want to come in with me?"

She thought about it for all of two seconds. "Yes, I do. I've never tagged along on a condom shopping trip."

"Don't tell me that's on your list."

"No, but maybe it should have been."

Rafe sighed and shook his head. "I'm not planning to linger over the selection, but if you want the experience, I'm not about to deprive you."

Moments later, Meg stood in front of the display while Rafe searched for the type he preferred. "It's been a while since I've looked at these," she said. "I had no idea there were so many different kinds."

"This is an especially well-stocked store," Rafe said. "Ah, there they are." He unhooked a package from a metal display rod.

"What did you get?" She glanced at the package. "Those don't look very interesting. Don't you want ones with ribs?"

He glanced at her with a grin. "I don't. Do you?"

"I'm not sure." She lowered her voice. "I've never had ribs before. At least I don't think I have. Are ribs a good idea?"

"Once again, I'm the wrong person to ask. They aren't going to do anything for me, but apparently they're supposed to provide an extra thrill for you. If you want me to get ribs, I will."

"Nah." She linked her arm through his and drew him

away from the condom display. "We'll save that for another time, after the regular ones become too boring."

He choked on a laugh. "If I have anything to do with it, the regular ones aren't going to be boring."

"I believe you'll have a great deal to do with it."

"I plan to, although we can't count out the malachite. In fact, from a scientific standpoint, we shouldn't add in another variable like ribs when we're testing the influence of the stone."

She paused, and since they were linked arm in arm, he had to stop, too. "Exactly how do you think the malachite is going to influence things, by the way?"

"Isn't it obvious?"

"Not to me."

"If you wear the necklace while we're having sex, then—"

"You want me to do that?"

He gazed down at her. "I've been imagining that ever since you put on the necklace. I thought you'd probably figured that out."

"No, I didn't." But now that he'd introduced the idea, she found herself becoming aroused by the mental picture he'd painted. "So this necklace isn't strictly for me, after all, is it?"

"No. It's along the lines of the vest you wanted me to buy."

She blew out a breath. "I feel *so* much better about accepting it now. Here I thought you were just buying me expensive jewelry, but you really wanted an accessory for your sexual fantasy."

He frowned. "That's not my *only* motivation. Once Samuel explained how he'd made the necklace for someone like you, I thought it would be a crime if you didn't own it."

"That's nice, too, but knowing you're thinking of some hot sexual scenario connected with it takes away my misgivings. In a sense, this necklace is as much for you as it is for me."

"Yeah." His gaze traveled from her mouth to her throat, down to the necklace, and beyond, to the cleavage she'd revealed by unfastening one more button.

The heat of that gaze made her shiver with longing. "Too bad we have to go through the whole dinner ritual."

"I know. I'm way hungrier for you than I am for food right now." And that hunger was obvious in his expression. "But we're here because of a family wedding, and that has to take priority over everything else."

She nodded as they continued up the aisle toward the cashier. "So let's get ourselves back to the ranch and be sociable. I'm trying to remember who's supposed to be at dinner tonight."

"A smaller group than we had last night, according to Sarah." Rafe paid for the box of condoms as nonchalantly as he might pay for a package of Life Savers.

Meg was impressed with his sophistication. She didn't know many guys who would be comfortable taking a woman in with them while they shopped for birth control. Rafe might have balked at the idea of buying clothing when she was along, but he had plenty of confidence when it came to anything sexual. She found that very arousing.

As they started back to the ranch, she began to count the days they'd have left before the wedding consumed all their time. "When's your dad flying in?"

"Thursday. I'm picking him up at the airport, which is one reason I rented the Lexus. He's partial to this make of car."

She sensed the eagerness to please in Rafe's voice. He wanted his father's approval and wasn't always sure he'd get it. "And Thursday night's the party at the Spirits and Spurs. Will he come to that?"

"I suppose. It's not going to involve strippers and raunchy movies, so he'll probably go."

"That's good. We'll have drinks and dancing. He should enjoy it."

"What kind of dancing?"

"Oh." She realized that it might not be quite the type his father would want. "Country, I'm afraid. The first night I was here, we all went into the Spirits and Spurs because they had a local band playing. It was a lot of fun, but it's definitely country music, and country swing is popular around here. Line dancing, too."

"He won't do any of that."

Meg took note of the finality in Rafe's statement. "You're sure? I mean, maybe if we get a couple of drinks in him, and one of the women who's really good at it coaxes him out on the floor, he'll—"

"It's not going to happen, Meg. Fact is, I don't know how to dance that way, either. I'll probably sit it out with my dad."

"I certainly hope not!"

He glanced at her in obvious surprise. "What's so wrong about that?"

"You're the best man, Rafe, so you can't just sit it out, even if your dad chooses to. Besides, the party is only the beginning. They'll have a DJ playing country music at the reception, too. It's part of your job to be out there on the dance floor."

"I hadn't thought of that. And Wyatt didn't say a word."

"I'm sure it's not one of the main things he's worried about, but I happen to think it's important. And if I have to appeal to your competitive instinct, I will. The Chance men have a reputation for being great dancers."

Rafe groaned. "This is not a hurdle I anticipated. Do you know anything about country swing or line dancing?"

"Some. But the best dancer in the family is Jack. If you really want to learn how to—"

"Are you seriously suggesting I ask Jack to teach me to dance?"

"I don't know. Maybe. Yes, I think I am. In fact, it would be excellent if Jack taught you to dance." She looked over at him and his jaw had tightened along with his grip on the steering wheel. "But you don't think so, do you?"

"Not so much."

"How much dancing experience do you have, exactly?"

"I…um…you know. Dancing at clubs."

"You mean where you get out on the floor and gyrate around without actually touching your partner?"

"Like that, yeah. I've done a little ballroom dancing, too."

She knew this would be a tough sell, but if she could convince him, he'd be much happier during the wedding festivities. "That's not quite the same thing. But I promise you, if you take on this challenge and master the Texas Two-Step and a couple of line dances, you'll be a hero."

"I will?" He sounded a little more interested.

"Guaranteed."

"I'm not saying I won't try, because I see your point. It's part of the festivities, and it'll look bad if I don't participate, but...Jack? Couldn't I learn from someone else?"

"You could, but after all, he is your brother."

"Half brother."

"Half brother, then. But let's say you get someone else to teach you, somebody on the ranch, maybe even Sarah. I've seen her dance with Jack and she's very good."

He nodded enthusiastically. "I'll ask Sarah. We get along great. She's a very kind woman, and besides, she is, in fact, a *woman*. Learning to dance from somebody of the opposite sex would be a plus."

"Yes, but think of the result. You'll show up at the party Thursday night with some skills you've learned from Sarah. But everyone knows Jack is the ultimate authority on country dancing, and they'll realize you wimped out and chose Sarah. You didn't go to The Man."

"I don't want to go to *The Man,* okay?"

"I'm telling you, Rafe, you'd score more points if you did. Jack's the best, and if you acknowledge that by asking for his help, he'll be proud of what you accomplish. You'll have an ally out on the floor instead of a competitor."

His jaw tightened again. "I don't care if Jack's an ally or not. I didn't come to the Last Chance to kiss up to my half brother."

Men. "I know you didn't! But can't you play the game, just for this week?"

"I'm still trying to picture me going up to Jack and asking if he'll teach me to dance. How am I supposed to do that with a straight face?"

"I'll go with you. I'm fairly sure that Jack, Josie and little Archie are coming to dinner tonight. It'll be your perfect opportunity."

"I don't know, Meg. Sounds like a disaster in the making."

"Rafe, if you'll take this on, I promise to dance with you a whole lot, both on Thursday night and Saturday night."

He was silent for a few seconds. "I hadn't thought of that. I don't want you out there dancing without me."

"Of course you don't, especially if I'm wearing this necklace and feeling all uninhibited."

He groaned. "All right. If Jack is there, I'll ask him. Jesus. I can't believe I just agreed to do that."

"You won't be sorry."

"I'm already sorry."

Meg smiled to herself. This week was turning out to be the most interesting one of her life.

11

Rafe prayed that Meg had been wrong and Jack wouldn't be coming to dinner, after all. But his luck didn't hold out. Jack, Josie and their seven-month-old son, Archie, sat down at the family dining table, along with Josie's brother Alex, who was the marketing director for the ranch, and his wife, Tyler, who organized seasonal events for the town of Shoshone.

Rafe was glad to meet Alex and Tyler, who hadn't made it the night before. He could see the family resemblance between Alex and Josie, who were both tall and blond. Tyler was a little brunette firecracker who used to work as a cruise ship activities director.

Tyler would be another good candidate as a dance teacher, Rafe thought. In fact, almost anybody would be better for the job than Jack Chance, in Rafe's opinion.

As they all gathered, Sarah explained that Nick and Dominique, along with Lester, were working on a framing project for Dominique's new show opening next week and couldn't take time to come up to the house for dinner. Wyatt and Olivia were in town visiting Olivia's father, an inventor who had a new gizmo to show them. Sarah's other daughter-in-law, Morgan, thought that she was catching a cold, so Gabe was home feeding her chicken soup and making sure little Sarah Bianca didn't get sick, too.

Rafe didn't wish sickness on anyone, but he wouldn't have minded if Jack had caught a cold instead of Morgan. While Rafe listened with half an ear to the dinner chitchat, he pictured Jack doubling over in a fit of laughter when he heard Rafe's request. That malachite stone Meg wore must have messed with his brain or he never would have agreed to this.

Everyone at the table admired the necklace, of course, and Rafe could feel speculation coming from all quarters. This family would understand what a necklace from Silver Reflections was worth, and the fact he'd bought it for Meg made a definite statement about how he felt toward her. He hadn't factored that in, but he still didn't regret buying it.

No, he only had one regret at the moment, and that was his idiotic promise to ask Jack to turn him into a twinkle toes on the dance floor. Sheesh. If only he could hit the delete button on that part of today's conversation with Meg.

She wasn't likely to let him off the hook, either. After only knowing her a short time, he realized that she was one determined woman. But he procrastinated all through dinner in hopes that maybe, after a glass of wine, she'd decide not to force the issue. Dessert was nearly over, and he was beginning to think maybe he'd avoid this humiliation, after all.

Then Alex, who was once a DJ and would perform that job during the reception, turned the conversation in a direction that was sure to cause Rafe trouble. "I'm still working on the playlist for Saturday night," Alex said. "I'm going for a mix of tunes because we'll have all ages there, and I've already consulted with Olivia and Wyatt on their favorites. But I'll take requests from this group, too."

"I hope you'll play 'Electric Boogie,'" Meg said. "The Electric Slide is the one line dance I've totally figured out."

"Already included," Alex said. "It's a classic and a crowd pleaser. Anything else?"

"'This Kiss' by Faith Hill," Josie said. "I love dancing with Jack to that song."

"Speaking of that," Meg said.

Rafe held his breath. *Here it comes.*

"Rafe and I were talking about the whole dancing thing, and it turns out he isn't all that familiar with country dancing. Jack's the expert in the family, so—"

"So," Rafe said, interrupting her, "I'd appreciate it, Jack, if you'd give me some pointers." If he had to do this, he might as well man up and ask the question himself.

For a split second everyone at the table was completely silent. In that split second Rafe began to sweat bullets.

"Be glad to," Jack said. His eyes crinkled at the corners as if he wanted to laugh, but to his credit, he didn't. "No time like the present." He pushed back his chair. "Let's head for the living room and move some furniture. I suggest we start with the Electric Slide."

At that moment Mary Lou, the ranch cook, bustled into the dining room with a carafe in her hand. "Who needs more coffee?"

Jack stood. "You know what, Mary Lou? Instead

of coffee, Rafe and I could use a six-pack of beer. I'm about to teach him to dance."

The cook stopped in her tracks. A fiftysomething woman with flyaway gray hair, she'd recently married a ranch hand who went by the single name of Watkins. "Let me get Watkins," she said. "He's gotta see this."

"No bystanders," Jack said. "Anybody who shows up in the living room has to dance."

Rafe sent Jack a look of gratitude. A lesson would be tough enough without an audience.

Mary Lou grinned. "No problem. Watkins is one hell of a dancer."

"I can do the footwork while I'm holding Archie." Josie extricated the baby from his high chair. "Is that good enough, Mr. Dance Instructor?"

Jack smiled at her. "You bet."

"That's great," Josie said, "because I wouldn't miss this for the world."

"I'm in," Alex said. "And, Rafe, buddy, I feel your pain. I didn't know squat about this stuff when I came here from Chicago two years ago."

Jack laughed. "And despite our best efforts, he still resists adopting the country way."

"Alex is an awesome dancer," Tyler said. "He just marches to a different drummer."

"Yeah." Josie winked at her brother. "I think it's that Animal dude from *The Muppet Show*."

"Nice, sis." Alex made a face at Josie.

Rafe glanced across the table. "Take heart, Alex. There's a new city boy in town."

"You'll be fine," Jack said. "Especially if Mary Lou remembers to bring us some beer."

Ten minutes later, a space in the living room had

been cleared of chairs, end tables and lamps. Music was arranged with help from a set of speakers out of Sarah's bedroom, and Josie contributed her downloaded tunes.

While Sarah and Josie searched for "Electric Boogie" on Josie's iPod, Rafe accepted the beer Jack handed him and took several healthy swallows.

"I have to say, I admire your guts," Jack said. "It's not easy to come into this situation as a greenhorn."

"Thanks, and no, it's not."

"Wyatt warned me that this kind of life isn't your style and you might be standoffish."

Rafe met his gaze. Each time he looked at Jack, he had the eerie sensation he was looking in a mirror. "To be honest, that was my original plan. It hasn't worked out that way."

Jack glanced over at Meg, who was practicing some line dancing steps with Tyler. "Women have a way of changing things."

"Yeah." Rafe drank some more beer.

"That's a nice necklace you bought her."

Rafe shrugged. "Well, like she said at dinner, it's her birthstone." He knew that was a really lame excuse for such an extravagant purchase, but he wasn't going into any more detail with Jack.

"Hey, I'm not questioning the decision. I've made a damned fool of myself over Josie plenty of times. Once you feel that connection, it's all over."

Rafe shook his head. "It's not like that with us."

"Not like what?"

"Neither one of us is looking for anything permanent."

"I see." Jack took a sip of his beer before glancing over at Rafe. "Let me get this straight. You're not interested in a commitment, but you bought her a valuable necklace that she'll cherish for the rest of her life. I have to tell you, that's…"

"Stupid?"

"I wasn't going to say that, but it makes no sense whatsoever."

"I know."

Jack laughed and clapped him on the back. "At least you admit that you're totally screwed. Come on, let's dance."

After one more fortifying swig of his beer, Rafe lined up between Meg and Tyler, with Alex on Tyler's far side and Mary Lou beside Alex. Jack, Josie, Sarah and her fiancé, Pete, stood in front of them, along with Mary Lou's new husband, Watkins, a barrel-chested guy with a handlebar mustache.

"We'll walk it through without music first," Jack said. "Rafe, copy what I do when you can see me, but there's turning involved, so sometimes you'll have to be copying Meg or Tyler."

"Don't copy me," Meg said. "I've been responsible for several Electric Slide train wrecks."

"That information does nothing to raise my confidence." Rafe tried not to anticipate disaster as he listened to Jack's instructions. Then he stumbled his way through something called a grapevine step. The forward and back part wasn't too bad, and eventually he had a general idea of which way to pivot and when to stomp and clap. But when Sarah switched on the music, everything he'd learned disappeared from his brain.

Watching Meg move through the steps and wiggle her adorable ass didn't help his concentration, either. Bumping into her and then slamming into Tyler was bad enough, but colliding head-on with Jack so that they practically embraced was damned embarrassing. Before the song was over, he'd managed to step on every set of toes within range at least once.

"Well, that wasn't too bad," Jack said. "Let's take a beer break and try it again."

"Great idea." Rafe located his beer and drained the bottle. When he came up for air, there was Meg, smiling at him.

"See? You're doing it."

"If you mean making a fool of myself, then yes, ma'am, I certainly am."

"No, you're not. You did great for your first time. One more run-through and you'll have it."

"You sure look good out there. You have a great sense of rhythm." He was trying desperately not to imagine how that would translate to sex. That thought had the power to derail him completely.

Her pink cheeks turned even pinker. "Thanks, but I still have to think about every step. I'll be glad when it's automatic and I can just go with the music."

"Everybody back in line," Jack called out. "We have a lot more work ahead of us."

Rafe took his position and mentally reviewed the steps the way he used to when he was first learning karate. As he did that, something clicked in his brain. Suddenly the movements fell into a logical pattern, one he could execute with barely a misstep, just as he'd done with karate.

When the music ended, Jack stuck his thumbs in his belt loops and surveyed Rafe with obvious satisfaction. "Either I'm a hell of a teacher, or you're a hell of a pupil. That's the fastest I've ever seen anyone learn a line dance."

Rafe couldn't help smiling. "Thanks."

"Don't go getting all full of yourself, though. That was the easy part. Next you're going to learn the Texas Two-Step, and that's a whole other ball game."

Sarah glanced at Jack. "Want me to be Rafe's partner?"

"No." A look of pure devilment lit Jack's eyes. "He'll learn faster if I'm his partner."

Rafe's smile faded. "I think I need another beer."

MEG HAD BEEN IMPRESSED with Rafe's willingness to stumble through a line dance until he caught on, but she'd expected him to balk at Jack's plan to partner him in the two-step.

Instead he took a couple of swallows of beer and then walked over to stand in front of Jack, arms spread. "I'm all yours."

"Lucky me." But Jack looked at Rafe with a new gleam of respect in his dark eyes. Meg had the feeling he was testing his half brother to see what he was made of.

"Okay, here's how we'll do it," Jack said. "I'm going to take the woman's part and you'll take the man's. Have you done any ballroom dancing?"

Rafe nodded. "Some."

"Then you know how that works. You lead and I follow. Here's your basic step." He moved through it as Rafe watched his feet. "Got that?"

"One more time."

Jack repeated the steps. "Okay?"

"Yep. Got it." His expression was completely deadpan as he gazed at Jack. "May I have this dance, you gorgeous thing?"

Jack grinned. "Just keep your hands where they belong, cowboy. I may be gorgeous, but I'm not easy. Mom, start the music."

Sarah was laughing so hard she had trouble getting the music going, but eventually a country tune filled the living room. Meg stared in fascination as Rafe placed his right hand at Jack's waist and Jack rested his left hand on Rafe's shoulder. Then they joined their right and left hands together and began to dance.

By rights, Rafe should have had to look down at his feet, but instead he kept his attention on Jack's face as the two men moved smoothly around the room.

"Woo!" Josie called out. "Sign these guys up for *Dancing with the Stars*."

"Hey," Alex said. "That looks like fun. Can I cut in?"

Jack started to laugh. "Dream on, Alex."

"Now I'm feeling jealous," Watkins said. "You've never asked me to dance, Jack. For all you know, I could be your ideal partner."

"Back off, you guys," Rafe said. "Jack's with me."

After that comment, Jack totally lost it. The two men staggered away from each other doubled over with laughter. Then Alex started dancing with Watkins, and the women paired up, too. By the end of the song, everyone was gasping for breath and wiping tears from their eyes.

Meg ended up dancing with Tyler, and after the music stopped, Tyler gave her a hug. "That was hysterical. You put Rafe up to that, didn't you?"

"I suggested he might ask Jack to teach him, but I never envisioned Jack actually dancing *with* him."

"Didn't surprise me at all. When I first met Jack he was kind of a stick-in-the-mud, but everyone told me he used to be a real character. He seems back to his old self these days."

"Obviously. I think I'm in love with this family."

"How could you not be? I thank my lucky stars that I met Alex and then had the good sense to give up the cruise business and settle down here with him."

"Do I remember right that you two have a house on Chance land?"

"We do." Tyler's dark eyes sparkled. "Sarah thinks of Alex as one of her sons, and she insisted that we should live out here, especially because Alex is such a big part of the marketing end of the business. I wasn't about to object to having a house built here. It's beautiful, and it's almost like our own little community since Jack, Gabe and Nick all have houses on the property, too."

Meg checked to see if Sarah was within earshot. "Olivia said Sarah wanted to deed some land over to Wyatt, but he said no."

"Yeah, that's right. I can understand it. He's so afraid someone will think he came here to cash in on the Chance money. Besides, Olivia has that cute little house in Shoshone, and her dad's right around the corner. I think she wants to stay in town."

"If I were in her shoes, I'd want to be out here," Meg said. "There's something magical about this ranch."

"I agree."

"And yet Rafe and Wyatt's mother—Jack's mother, too, come to think of it—couldn't wait to give it up." Meg shook her head. "I don't understand that."

"So have you heard anything? Is she coming to the wedding?"

"I don't think Rafe knows. I don't think anyone knows. I hate that she's holding everybody hostage like this."

"From what I've heard, she's not a very nice person."

"And yet her sons are terrific." Meg glanced over at Rafe, who was drinking beer and laughing with Jack. "I don't know what's for the best, but everyone's getting along so well. It almost seems better if she doesn't show up. I can picture her ruining everything."

12

DESPITE HAVING A GREAT TIME with Jack and the others, Rafe kept thinking about his plans for tonight, which didn't include anyone except Meg. But they had to wait for the evening to wind down. They couldn't exactly announce that they were going upstairs…together.

After all the talk about the necklace, especially his conversation with Jack, Rafe didn't have any illusions about what the family suspected. Nobody would be the least bit surprised to know what Rafe had in mind once everyone retired for the evening. He didn't really care if they knew.

But he kept thinking about Jack's response to the situation. Jack was convinced that Rafe and Meg were headed for some kind of happily-ever-after. Glancing around the room, Rafe could see why he would think so.

Everywhere Rafe looked were happy couples—Jack and Josie, Alex and Tyler, Mary Lou and Watkins, Sarah and Pete. The Last Chance seemed to foster healthy, loving relationships, except in one significant case. His mother had not been blissfully happy here.

Rafe couldn't regret that, because if she'd stayed with

Jonathan Chance, he and Wyatt wouldn't exist. Still, he wondered what would happen if Diana, who was extremely high maintenance, descended on the festivities. Sad to say, he couldn't see a good outcome.

At long last, the gathering began to break up. Alex and Tyler left first. Then Jack and Josie started gathering Archie's baby stuff. Sarah asked to hold Archie one last time, and Jack walked over and held out his hand to Rafe.

"You've been a good sport." His grip was firm. "I had my doubts about you when you drove up in that fancy-dancy car, but I think you're going to be okay."

"Thanks. And thanks for being my dance instructor tonight."

Jack grinned. "That will go down in the annals of the family history, my friend. Just so you know, I've never danced with a guy before in my life."

"Couldn't prove it by me. You seemed totally relaxed about it."

"I wanted to see what you'd do if I suggested it."

"And?"

"And you called my bluff. That always gets my attention." He clapped Rafe on the shoulder. "Welcome to the family, little brother."

To Rafe's surprise and embarrassment, his throat closed up with emotion. He coughed to cover it. "I'm glad to be here."

"You haven't heard anything from Diana, right?"

"Nothing."

"You'll tell me if you do, I hope."

Rafe nodded. "You'll be the first to know. No, cancel that. You'll be the second to know. If I hear something, I have to make sure Wyatt's aware."

Jack sighed. "In some ways I'd like her to show up and get the drama out of the way. But it could be a real rodeo if she does."

"Not if I have anything to say about it."

Jack's eyebrows lifted. "You'd run interference?"

"Of course."

"Good man." He gave Rafe's shoulder another squeeze. "See you at the party Thursday night. Wear your dancing shoes." With a wink, he turned to walk with Josie out the front door.

"That's about all the fun Watkins and I can take for one night," Mary Lou said. "We have a little tidying up in the kitchen, and then we're off to bed."

Sarah yawned and stretched. "I think Pete and I are ready to pack it in, too." She glanced over at Rafe. "You were terrific tonight. I haven't seen Jack laugh that hard in a long time. It did my heart good to see you two getting along so well."

"The credit belongs to Wyatt," Rafe said. "He's the one who broke the ice and made sure that we got to know our half brother."

Sarah's expression softened. "He did, at that. He's a very special guy. He and Olivia have a bright future."

"They do." As Rafe said that, he felt a pang of envy. Wyatt had found a woman who wanted to spend a lifetime with him and they were about to start that journey together.

A couple of days ago, before Rafe had met Meg, he had thought settling down was a long way off for him. But since then he'd experienced life in a whole new way. Instead of being constantly focused on his career and the bottom line, he'd started thinking about how he would spend the money he was accumulating.

He'd had no particular plan other than becoming wealthy enough that he wouldn't have to worry about his future. But besides being a rich man, how did he visualize that future? He realized now that he'd never created a detailed picture of what he wanted. Or who he wanted to be there with him.

His attention wandered, as it had all evening, to Meg. She was so full of life. Anyone lucky enough to spend time in her presence would find her a constant source of energy and inspiration. Yeah, she threw him off balance a lot, and he was learning to enjoy the slightly dizzy feeling that came from taking crazy chances.

"I think it's wonderful that you and Meg have discovered that you're kindred spirits," Sarah said. "That makes it very convenient, doesn't it, since Meg and Olivia are such good friends?"

Rafe thought of contradicting Sarah's assumption the way he'd contradicted Jack earlier. He couldn't bring himself to do it. "It does make it nice," he said.

"You have very good taste."

"You mean the necklace?"

"No, the woman." Sarah gave him a hug. "Be happy, Rafe. Oh, and turn out the lights before you go up to bed, okay?"

"Sure."

With one last smile in his direction, she linked arms with Pete and they walked down the hallway toward her bedroom.

Rafe watched them go. He couldn't remember the last time his mother had hugged him. Sarah had known him a very short time, and yet she'd embraced him with warmth and affection, as if he were a long-lost son. For the second time tonight, Rafe found his chest tightening with emotions he wasn't used to feeling.

"Looks like everyone's going to bed."

He turned around at the sound of Meg's voice, which held a soft purr of sensuality that made his blood sing.

She stood a couple of feet away looking incredibly beautiful. The lamplight on her fiery hair created an angelic halo, but her expression wasn't the least bit angelic. Her green gaze burned with earthly lust.

"How about you?" Heart thumping, he eliminated the distance between them and drew her close. Her heat fueled his fantasies. "Are you ready for bed?"

She smiled and wrapped her arms around his neck. "I've been ready for bed for hours."

He welcomed the warmth of her arms at the back of his neck. "Me, too. I thought the evening was going to last forever."

"Same here." She wiggled closer. "But it was good, even if I was impatient to be alone with you."

His breath caught as she aligned her body with his. He tightened his grip, and allowed his gaze to travel downward, past the polished silver and malachite to the shadowed treasures beyond. The return journey brought him back to her incredible eyes. "It *was* good. Thank you, Meg. If you hadn't challenged me to try the whole dance thing, tonight wouldn't have turned out so well."

"I noticed that you and Jack had a few words before he left."

"We did." He savored this moment of holding her close, knowing that soon, they would be closer yet. Anticipation built, teasing him with possibilities. "As you predicted, we're allies now. And that's important considering what may happen this week."

Sympathy flashed in her eyes. "Your mother."

"Yes. But now Jack and I, and Wyatt, too, for that matter, can present a united front if she does show up. Without this wild dance lesson, I don't know if that would have been possible." He reached up and caressed her cheek. "And it's all because of you."

"No. You had to actually follow through. What you did tonight required a lot of courage. Now that it's behind you, you might not think so, but—"

"Oh, it required a lot of courage. I'm not about to minimize that. I was nervous as hell." He stroked his thumb across her cheekbone. All the lipstick was gone from her pink mouth. It looked even sexier bare. "But as I'm learning from you, these are the risks worth taking, aren't they?"

"I think so."

"Proud of me?"

"Yes, I am."

"Good." His pulse rate skyrocketed as he leaned down and brushed his mouth over her pink, smiling lips. "Because it's time for me to claim my reward."

"Finally." Spinning out of his arms, she grabbed his hand and pulled. "Come on, Locke. We have a date."

Laughing, he ran with her up the stairs. Briefly he remembered that he was supposed to douse the lights. Oh, hell, he'd do it later. A hot woman was dragging him off to bed. A guy didn't stop to turn off lights at a time like that.

She dashed through his bedroom door first, and he barely had time to kick it closed before she leaped on him. Wrapping her arms around his neck and her legs around his waist, she grinned at him. "I hope you know where your condoms are, big boy."

Cupping his hands under her perfect little ass, he carried her to the bed, kissing her cheeks, her nose, her mouth. "I know exactly where they are, sweet stuff." He'd left on a bedside lamp in anticipation of this moment. "Time to get you naked so I can use one."

"I can hardly wait."

Neither could he, and judging from the pressure under his fly, he'd have a devil of a time holding off long enough to give her a good time. But he would do it because she deserved no less.

Depositing her on the bed, he followed her down. Ah, glorious. He loved having his arms full of Meg. His feet were still on the floor, but he couldn't be bothered with taking off his boots right now. He had a blouse to unbutton. Leaning over her, he started in on that job while continuing to kiss and nibble at her plump mouth.

"Too slow," she said between kisses as she pushed his hands away. "Let me."

"Then I'll work on your jeans."

"No." She struggled for breath. "You work on *your* jeans."

His breathing wasn't any steadier than hers, and his heart hammered like a car about to throw a rod. "Bossy, aren't you?"

She laughed and gulped for air. "Horny."

"That's my good luck." The blood pounded in his ears as he unbuckled and unzipped. He had to interrupt his assignment when her jeans got stuck on her shoes. Kneeling, he pulled off both shoes and then figured he might as well finish the operation and tugged off her jeans and panties, too.

"Almost done." She whipped off her blouse, tossed

it aside, unhooked her bra, and threw it on top of the blouse. "There." She leaned back on her elbows.

He went still. She was a work of art, and no matter how bossy she tried to be, he would take time to pay homage. Her breasts were lush—round and smooth, tempting him with wine-dark nipples. They were generous in comparison to her slender torso and narrow waist. The silver necklace gleamed against her bare skin.

His cock throbbed as his gaze swept over the sweet curve of her hips, the graceful length of her slim legs and the fiery patch of curls between her thighs.

"Rafe," she murmured. "You're not moving."

"No. I'm looking."

"Me, too, or at least I'm trying to. The view is seriously obstructed. Would you please do something about that?"

"Yeah, sure." Not taking his eyes from her, he reached down and pulled off a boot, shifted his weight to the other leg and yanked off the second one, which fell with a thud to the floor.

She ran a tongue over her lips. "Your shirt."

"Right." Still watching her, he grabbed both sides of the shirt and pulled. The snaps gave way like exploding popcorn, and she laughed in a low, sexy voice that drove him crazy.

He started moving faster, dropping the shirt to the floor and shoving down his jeans and briefs. The belt buckle clattered to the floor as he stepped out of the whole shebang and kicked it aside.

She took a long, shaky breath as she gave him the same top-to-bottom scrutiny he'd given her. "Awesome." Her breasts quivered as she drew another breath. "Now bring that wonderful stuff over here, okay?" She parted her legs a fraction, in a subtle, yet tantalizing invitation. "I have a place you can put it."

He almost swallowed his tongue. Grabbing the handle on the bedside table drawer, he jerked it out with such force that the whole thing fell to the floor. He left it there, scooped up the box of condoms, and tore it open, destroying it in the process. Condoms flew everywhere.

But he only needed one, and he managed to get a good grip on it. His fingers shook as he tried to tear the foil. He'd never wanted a woman so much in his life.

"Here." She took it out of his hand and in two seconds had that little raincoat ready to put on.

He reached for it. "I'll—"

"No, *I'll*." Her gaze swept the length of his erect penis. "You wouldn't deprive a girl of dressing up something that beautiful, would you?"

"Meg, at this moment, I wouldn't deprive you of anything. If you wanted me to buy you the Taj Mahal, I'd…" He clenched his jaw as she rolled the condom on. He was so close. Too damned close.

"I don't want the Taj Mahal." Scooting back on the bed, she held out her arms. "I want you."

"That's good, because that's what you're about to get." He climbed onto the bed, grateful for the generous space that allowed them to lie across the mattress. That way he didn't have to take the time to change position.

As he looked into her eyes, he saw his urgency mirrored there. But if he responded to that, if he thrust deep as he longed to do and kept on pumping frantically, he'd come in seconds. "We're going to take this slow at first," he said.

She grasped his hips and lust blazed in her eyes. "What if I want fast and furious?"

"I can't. You've turned me on more than I can remember ever being turned on. My control is shot, and I want to make sure that you—"

"I feel as if I could come right this minute, just looking into your eyes."

"Me, too." He drew in a breath. "Which is why we're going to ease into the situation gradually." Bracing his arms on either side of her shoulders, he probed her moist heat gently with his cock.

She groaned. "You're teasing me."

"No." He fought the wave of his own climax. "I'm trying not to come. Help me."

"How?"

"Lie still."

Slowly she relaxed against the bed. "I'm still."

"Don't move."

"I won't."

He slid partway in. So good. Too good. He closed his eyes and slowly exhaled. There. Better.

"More." She sounded desperate.

Opening his eyes, he looked into hers and found the control he needed. "Yes, more." With one firm movement, he thrust home.

She gasped. Arching upward, she dug her fingers into his back. "Rafe, I'm…" With a soft wail, she came apart, shuddering against him, her spasms stroking his rock-hard cock.

Somehow he held on without coming, and as she began to drift down from the heights, he withdrew slightly and rocked forward again, making sure he pressed against her clit. Instantly she tensed again. Her eyes flew open and she looked up at him.

He smiled as he began a steady rhythm. "Let's try that again, shall we?"

"Oh." Wrapping her legs around his, she rose to meet each thrust. "Rafe, that's so… I can feel every… nerve ending… I…"

Gazing into her eyes, he soaked up the pleasure he could see there. Her breathless murmurs spurred him on to give her all he knew how to give. Shifting the angle slightly, he wondered if he could locate her G-spot.

When her pupils widened, he thought maybe he had. "Like that?"

"Uh-huh." She began to pant. "Certainly do. Oh, yeah. Magic…" She moaned softly with each stroke.

He pumped faster, and her moans grew in volume. He wasn't sure about the acoustics in this house, so he leaned down and covered her mouth with his. When she came again, he let himself come with her, and they swallowed each other's cries as they rode the wind together.

Gasping for breath, he lifted his head and gazed down at her in silent wonder. Making love to her had been everything he'd imagined it would be and more.

Her lashes fluttered, and she opened her eyes. A slow smile of satisfaction curved her kiss-reddened mouth. "That," she said, "was seriously good."

"Yes, it was." Her smile was contagious, and he hoped he wasn't grinning like an idiot. "So what do you think? Should we quit while we're ahead?" He thought he knew the answer, but it was fun to test her response.

"Are you insane? Now that I've got you in my clutches, I intend to wear you out."

"I was hoping you'd say that." Easing away from her, he crawled off the bed and grabbed a tissue to dispose of the condom. "Don't forget, you recommended a hot bath for my poor aching muscles."

She rose up on her elbows again. "I did, didn't I?"

"Think I'll go down the hall and run that bath right now."

"And leave me here sad and lonely?"

"Hell, no. I need someone to wash my back."

She glanced around the room. "No bathrobe."

"So what? Nobody's upstairs but us."

"Good point." Scooting out of bed, she stood beside him and laced her fingers through his. "Come along, cowboy. Let's have us some nice clean fun."

13

FORTUNATELY THE TUB WAS the old-fashioned kind, which made it almost big enough for two if they were willing to get cozy. Meg was more than willing to do that. She hoped that she wasn't being too obvious ogling Rafe's body, but he was one ripped dude.

As the water ran into the tub, she stroked a hand down his biceps. "I assume you got this way because you work out."

"Nah, I was born like this."

"Must have been rough on your mother." She'd meant it as a joke, but immediately she regretted bringing up the subject of Diana. "Sorry. Cancel that remark."

"It's okay." He pulled her into his arms. "I've had to deal with her all my life. I figured out pretty early that she wasn't the poster girl for motherhood."

Meg nestled against his sculpted chest and enjoyed the growing evidence of his interest pressing against her belly. "Let's talk about your workouts." She glanced up at him. "Judging from the evidence—" she slid her hands up his muscled back "—you're in the gym a fair bit."

"I am." He cupped her bottom and brought her in close. "I work off a lot of stress there, but now that I've met you, I can imagine a much better way to do that."

She nodded. "Sex as a stress buster. I can go along with that idea."

"In fact, I wonder if you'd be willing to act as my safety valve if this wedding craziness gets out of hand."

"That conjures up some interesting scenarios." She rubbed languidly against him. "So let's say on Thursday night, the pressure gets too intense for one reason or another. Shall we meet in the backseat of your Lexus?"

He stroked upward and moved both hands around to fondle her breasts. "On the other hand, why wait for pressure to build up? Why don't we just plan on some backseat sex during the party?"

"You're a bad boy, Rafe Locke." She leaned into his caress and closed her eyes. "How's the water level?" she murmured.

"What water level? I— Yikes, the *water level*." Releasing her quickly, he spun toward the tub and turned off the faucet. "I'm going to drain some out. We don't want to flood the place when we both get in."

"And start splashing around."

He glanced over his shoulder. "Are you a splasher?"

"Depends on what's happening in the tub."

He gazed at her, amusement in his dark eyes. "Maybe I'll drain out a little bit more, then. I have some thoughts about what might be happening in the tub, and you might turn into a splasher, at that." He watched the water level and finally put the plug back in the drain. "That looks about right."

"Maybe you should get in by yourself for a while.

You really should soak your thigh muscles in warm water."

"That doesn't sound like any fun. I'll get in first, though, since I'll take up the most room. Then we'll work you in around me."

She glanced at the proud jut of his penis. "You'd take up less room if you could tame your friend, there."

"That's your department." He sat down in the tub, leaned back, and held out his hand. "Come on in. The water's fine."

"Just where do you intend to put me?" She'd thought they both might fit, but he really was bigger—in all respects—than she'd realized.

He drew his knees up slightly. "There's room at the far end."

"Let me take off my necklace first." She hadn't been without it since she'd first put it on this afternoon, and as she laid the silver spiral on the counter, she touched the malachite once for good luck. "Do you think I'll still be uninhibited if I'm not wearing it?"

"I don't know. Do you feel a lot different when it's on?"

She turned back to him with a smile. "Seeing you naked has a greater effect on my inhibitions than a piece of malachite ever could."

"Then we should join a nudist colony."

"Ah, but I don't want to share."

"Okay, then I'll have to remember to strip down whenever we're alone."

"Sounds good to me." She stepped into the small space he'd left her. "Okay, now what?"

"Sit down and stretch your legs out on each side of my hips."

Somehow she managed it. With her legs apart, the warm water caressed her intimately and she flushed as she felt the first tug of arousal.

"Okay, now hold my hands tight. I'm going to put my legs around you and pull you toward me. I'll do it slowly so we don't send waves crashing over the sides of the tub."

"I'm trying to imagine where this is going."

He laughed. "I'm not exactly sure. I'm making it up as I go along."

"That's not very comforting. What if we get twisted up in here and can't untangle without pulling a groin muscle?"

"I forgot to mention I was also on the wrestling team in high school. I can get us out of anything. Now slide forward. That's it. Closer, closer…there. How's that?"

"Interesting. Puts me in striking distance." She reached out and wrapped her hand around his cock, slick with water.

"Mmm." His gaze grew heavy-lidded as she caressed him. "So far, so good."

"I don't know what this is doing for your thighs."

"Who cares? And the beauty of this position is that it works both ways." Slipping his hand between her legs under the water, he rubbed his knuckle over her clit.

She drew in a quick breath as her womb twitched in reaction.

"I love watching how your eyes grow dark when you're excited."

"Who says I'm excited?"

"You're not? Then let's try this." Changing the position of his hand, he gently pushed two fingers into her slick channel, which was already starting to quiver.

His thumb rested lightly on her trigger point. Then he began to lazily stroke it back and forth as he found her G-spot with the pads of his fingers.

"Uh, that's pretty nice right there." Understatement of the year.

Then he stopped moving his hand.

"You could keep that up if you want."

"It's your turn."

"Oh." She was still holding his cock, but she'd forgotten about the caressing part. Squeezing lightly, she moved her hand up and down.

His breathing grew rougher. "If we were into delayed gratification, we could see how long we could keep this up, starting and stopping, without coming."

She continued to stroke him. "Are you into delayed gratification?"

"Maybe someday. Not tonight." He swallowed. "See if you can still do that while I…do this." He massaged her G-spot again.

The pleasure nearly made her lose her concentration, but she kept reminding herself to touch him, caress him and make him tremble the way he was making her tremble. She held his gaze. "Your eyes get dark, too."

"I'll bet." His breath came faster. "I'm getting close."

"Me, too." She slid her hand up and down faster as he increased the pace of his massage. Water sloshed back and forth, and the sound made the moment even more erotic.

"You're almost there. I can see it in your eyes."

"Yes." Her answer was breathless. "Can you…?"

"Almost. Faster. Don't be loud."

"I won't."

"That's it…good…good…now!" He pressed down on

her clit with his thumb and she came at the same moment his warm essence spilled over her hand.

As their breathing slowed and the water stopped churning, they sat there in a happy daze looking into each other's eyes, in no hurry to move. But at last she released him and he slowly withdrew his hand.

He cleared his throat. "Bet that wasn't on your list."

"No." She smiled at him. "But it should have been."

RAFE TOOK GREAT CARE in drying Meg after they climbed out of the bathtub. Then, because she'd remarked on his muscles and made him feel as if he should demonstrate his strength, he wrapped her in a towel, scooped her up and carried her back to the bedroom.

"I'm liking this." She looped her arms around his neck.

"When we get to the bed, I'm going to unroll you from the towel like Cleopatra was unrolled from a rug. Then I'm going to have my way with you, which is what a he-man does when he carts a woman off to his bed."

"Am I supposed to struggle and protest?"

He shrugged. "You can if that turns you on."

"Not particularly, but if it turns *you* on, I'll be happy to put up a token fight."

"I've never been into that. Too much work. I'd much rather have sex with a woman who's warm and juicy and willing."

"That describes me to a T."

"Then I think we're going to get along." He thought they were already getting along in a way that astounded him. It seemed as if he'd known Meg for years. He'd never put much stock in the concept of soul mates, but he was beginning to think there might be something to it.

Still, there were some inconvenient aspects to that theory. First of all, Meg had never said she was looking for a soul mate. Even if she were, he made his living, and a very good living, in San Francisco. She had talked about leaving Pittsburgh, but only because she wanted to relocate to Jackson Hole.

Maybe geography wasn't supposed to factor into this soul mate business, but he couldn't imagine having a soul mate who lived hundreds of miles away. He pictured a closer physical connection than that. Anyway, Meg had said she wasn't interested in settling down with one guy right now, so eventually he'd have to change her mind in addition to changing her location.

For now, though, she was the perfect person to help him through this wedding week, and he wasn't about to complain because he couldn't have more than that. So far his trip to Jackson Hole had turned out about five hundred percent better than he'd anticipated.

After carrying Meg into his bedroom, he shoved the door closed with his shoulder. Maybe it was a silly precaution since they were the only people upstairs, but with what he had in mind for the next few minutes, he thought a closed door was appropriate.

Depositing Meg on the edge of the bed, he grabbed the ends of the towel, pulled hard, and she tumbled out all pink and glowing from their bath and her orgasm. He wanted to keep that glow alive. Fortunately he thought he could. She was a very easy woman to please.

"I like this bed." She stretched her arms above her head.

"I like you in this bed." Lying down next to her, he

ran his hand from her throat downward, smoothing his palm over her breasts and pausing to tease her nipples until they stood erect.

"Is this what you mean by having your way with me?"

"It's a start." Rolling over so he was braced on top of her, he treated himself to some mouth-to-nipple stimulation. Sucking gently, he reached between her thighs and found her warm and juicy, just as she'd promised.

She began to moan and thrash beneath him. "I want you again. Maybe you should get another—"

"Not yet." He kissed her damp breasts and gave each pert nipple one last lick before he journeyed downward. "First I must have my way with you."

"I'm beginning to understand what you meant by that."

"Smart girl." He took his time getting to his destination. Her skin was tasty, and he loved running his tongue over it and feeling her shudder in response.

But at last he reached nirvana, the special place guarded by fiery curls. Nudging them aside, he settled in and laid siege to any last lingering inhibitions she might have had.

His first explorations were subtle. He used only the tip of his tongue and the faintest brush of his mouth. She sighed and relaxed, opening her thighs in surrender.

Excitement bloomed within him as he took advantage of that surrender. His next foray was deeper, more intense, and she gasped in reaction. But the moment to stop him had long passed. If she'd thought briefly of holding back, of denying him entrance to all that she was, it was too late.

He captured her fully then, using his tongue to lap

and thrust, his mouth to suck her juices until she grew wild with pleasure, rolling her hips so that he had to grasp them firmly and hold her still in order to love her. And when she was gasping and trembling, he loved her with even more enthusiasm, and she came in an unbidden rush, all her barriers gone as she flooded his taste buds with her ambrosia.

And because he couldn't resist, he made her come again, and when it was over, she lay spent, her arms flung out to her sides, her eyes glazed, her lips parted as she drew in quick, shallow breaths that made her body quiver and her breasts tremble.

Sliding up beside her, he pulled her against his hard body, his aroused and in-need-of-release body. But it was not the time. For now, he'd taken all she had to give, and it was enough. With a sigh, he closed his eyes, willed his erection to subside, and slept.

How long he slept, he had no idea. But he awoke to the sweet sensation of being aroused slowly and with great tenderness. She'd scooted down so she could kiss and lick his rapidly stiffening cock.

After the way he'd turned her inside out, he had no doubt she intended the same fate for him. But he wanted to love her the old-fashioned way one more time before the night was through.

Reaching down, he combed his fingers through her hair. "I need a condom."

"Not necessarily." She continued to stroke him, kiss him and fondle his balls.

He loved it, but he wanted that basic connection when he was buried up to the hilt and looking into her glorious eyes. "I want to be inside you, Meg. I need to be inside you."

She paused. "You do?"

"Yes, I do."

Wiggling up so that she could see his face, she gazed at him in puzzlement. "Why?"

"I don't know," he answered honestly. "I just need to be there."

"Okay. Hang on and I'll get a condom."

"Thank you." His groin ached for the climax she'd been working toward.

Leaning over him so that her breast dangled temptingly close to his mouth, she grabbed one of the scattered condoms from the floor.

He wanted to sample her breasts again, tuck his head between her thighs and taste the glory of her climax on his tongue. He didn't want the night to end…ever. But he knew it would soon.

Glancing down, he watched her roll on the condom. She was so earnest, so sexy, so completely right for him. He pushed that last thought away as he started to ease her to her back.

"Stay there," she murmured. "I think we can do it this way." Shifting into position, she hooked one leg over his hip. Facing him, she wiggled around and guided him in until they were locked together just as he'd wanted. "How's that?" She gripped his shoulder.

"I can't move much."

"You won't have to for my sake. I'm on this permanent sexual high. Touch me anywhere and I'll probably come."

"Really?" He spread his hand over the curve of her ass and squeezed. "Here?"

"Maybe."

Exploring this interesting connection between them, he stroked the spot right where they were joined.

She shivered.

He stroked it again as he began to pump gently into her, and she drew in a quick breath. How he loved watching her eyes as her climax hovered ever nearer. He couldn't imagine growing tired of the thrill.

Moving faster now, he put more pressure on that sensitive spot that seemed to give her pleasure.

She held his gaze and tightened her grip on his shoulders.

"Come for me, Meg."

"As if I could help it." Her breath grew ragged.

He touched her there again, and being able to feel the vibration of his cock moving in and out sent his system into meltdown, too. His balls tightened, readying for the surge of ecstasy.

She gulped. "I'm there."

"I know." Pressing hard with his finger, he drove into her and she cried out his name as she tumbled into the abyss.

One more thrust, and he tumbled with her, calling for her, needing her. He no longer cared if someone heard. All that mattered was the joy that blotted out everything. Without knowing it, he'd searched all his life for that all-consuming joy.

He wouldn't expect it to last. Nothing ever did. But for now it was his, and he would take it and be grateful.

14

MEG AWOKE BEFORE SUNRISE feeling sore but happy. No man had loved her like that since...ever. She'd never had a lover to compare with Rafe. That didn't mean she would tell him so, because he might think she was going ape-shit over him and that might scare him off.

She wasn't sure what she wanted to do about Rafe, but she definitely didn't want to scare him off. Nor was she going to get all weird on him and slip out of bed while he was still asleep, leaving him to wonder about her state of mind.

No, they would face this morning together and make sure they were both okay with everything before they headed downstairs to greet what would probably be curious stares. She wasn't too worried about that. From what she could tell, the Last Chance had seen its share of romances over the years.

Whatever was going on between her and Rafe might not be a permanent thing, but it was definitely a romance. They'd fallen asleep facing each other, holding hands. They'd both agreed that the old spooning position that seemed so popular didn't give either of them room to move around. She thought his willingness to give her space, even as they fell asleep, was significant.

During the night they'd relaxed and sought their own familiar sleeping positions. She lay on her back, gazing up at the beamed ceiling, and he was sprawled on his stomach, the pillow bunched under his head, and his eyes closed. She listened to his even breathing and remembered how that breathing changed when he was loving her. She'd have plenty of memories to keep her warm after this week ended.

"I can hear you thinking over there." Rafe's voice was rough with sleep, but tender, too.

She rolled to face him. "I couldn't tell if you were awake."

"I'm awake, and I have a blasted erection, which makes no sense after the night we had. I should be limp as a shredded bike tire, but I'm…not." With his morning stubble and the gleam of lust in his dark eyes, he looked even more like a bad boy.

"Yeah, but mornings are supposed to be a guy's best time, aren't they?"

His lips curved in a bad-boy smile. "I tried like hell to give you my best last night."

"And I have no complaints." She stroked his bristly cheek. "But since I'm still here, there's no reason for you to suffer."

"Noble of you, Nurse Meg."

"I'm only happy to serve. Roll over so I can check your condition."

"Oh, boy." He rolled to his back and displayed his stiff penis. "Doctor was always my favorite game."

"Mmm. You do seem to have a condition. Major

swelling going on." She tapped his shaft with her finger. "Does that hurt?"

"Only when you stop."

"I suggest covering it with a latex membrane to contain the swelling."

"What a coincidence." He leaned over and snagged a condom packet from the floor. "I happen to have that very thing lying around."

"Lucky for you." She ripped open the packet.

"Tell me about it, Nurse Meg."

"Now lie still while I apply the latex."

"Yes, ma'am."

"You may be a bit uncomfortable at first…"

"No kidding." He gritted his teeth as she slowly rolled on the condom. "Could you possibly speed it up a little?"

"I like to take my time with my patients."

"That's all well and good, but…ahh…whatever you're doing with your pinky fingers is not helping."

She struggled not to laugh. "Am I doing something with my pinky fingers? Oh, dear, the swelling seems to be getting worse. And your breathing is very irregular. I think you need some mouth-to-mouth resuscitation." Straddling him carefully so that she didn't touch his cock at all, she leaned down and kissed him on the mouth, with plenty of tongue.

He moaned and grasped her hips, trying to position her where he wanted her.

She wiggled free and sat down firmly on his thighs. Shaking her finger at him, she gave him a stern glance. "You're taking liberties, sir."

"And you're taking forever, Nurse Meg." He gestured

toward his condom-covered penis. "Are you going to reduce the swelling like you promised, or not?"

"Oh, all right." Sighing dramatically, she rose to her hands and knees. "Let's try some deep-tissue massage."

"Yeah, let's. The deeper the better." He bracketed her hips with both hands.

"Don't be hasty, now." Her little game was catching up with her. After so much foreplay, she wanted him as much as he wanted her. Her heart raced as she settled herself over the very tip of his rigid cock. But she couldn't resist teasing him by taking him in a millimeter at a time.

With a low growl he tightened his grip. "Enough's enough." He thrust upward, filling her in one swift movement.

She gasped with pleasure. "Sir!"

"Ah." He lowered his hips and pulled her down with him. "I feel better already."

Her body hummed with delight as the length and breadth of him touched her in all the right places. "I suppose we could try some patient-directed therapy."

His dark eyes glittered. "Such as?"

Leaning forward, she nibbled at his mouth. "Tell me how you want it, big boy."

His instructions were low and intense. "I want you to ride me, Nurse Meg. Ride me hard and fast."

Heat rocketed through her, igniting fires in every sensitive spot. "If you think you're up to it."

"I'll take my chances."

"Then here we go." She started off gradually, getting her bearings, finding her rhythm, but in seconds the power of being in control tempted her to pump faster.

He rose to meet her, his thighs slapping her bottom

with each stroke. The mattress shivered and shook as they came together in a wild frenzy of need.

He gasped for breath. "Meg...I can't wait..." With a groan, he drove into her and came.

She absorbed the spasms of his release and tightened the muscles holding him deep within her. She was close, so close. And then she felt his thumb press hard against her clit and she erupted, her climax dancing and twirling in time with his.

As the waves of pleasure subsided, she sank down onto his chest. They were both slick with sweat, and she rubbed back and forth to savor the feel of his moist chest hair lightly scratching her breasts.

He wrapped his arms around her and sighed. "I could stay in this bed with you all day, Nurse Meg."

"I must have a good bedside manner, then." She rested her cheek against his muscled shoulder.

"The best. There's no one I'd rather have tend to my swelling issues." He stroked her back. "Then again, the more I'm around you, the more swelling issues I seem to have, so it's possible you're both the cause and the cure."

"That works out rather neatly, don't you think?"

"It does, especially if we could escape to a deserted island right now."

"That does sound appealing. But there's this wedding on Saturday."

He sighed again. "I know."

"And in addition to the bride and groom, and the minister, of course, we're the other two most significant members of the wedding party."

"And maybe the most important thing to remember is this—if Wyatt hadn't decided to marry Olivia, chances are we would never have met."

"Oh." She lifted her head and met his gaze. "That's too terrible to contemplate."

"Yeah." He tunneled his fingers through her hair. "I wouldn't have known what I was missing, but I would have missed so much." He drew her toward him. "Your chin has a touch of whisker burn from your mouth-to-mouth resuscitation."

"I don't care."

"Good, because I want to kiss you once more before we climb out of this bed and get on with our day."

"Please do."

His lips found hers in the sweetest, most tender kiss he'd given her yet. She barely felt the prickle of his beard. It was the sort of loving kiss that she wished could go on much longer than it did.

When he pulled back, he looked into her eyes with the same sweet tenderness. "You're amazing," he said. "Thank you for giving me such an unforgettable night."

"I won't forget it, either," she said softly. "But I'm hoping for another invitation tonight."

"Consider yourself invited. It'll be the last time we're up here alone. My dad will be in a bedroom in your wing after that."

And maybe his mother, although she decided not to mention that possibility. "Then we'll just have to enjoy our privacy while we have it. And now, I'm heading back down to my own room." She extricated herself from his arms and climbed out of bed.

"I'm getting up, too." He left the bed and disposed of the condom.

Stooping, she gathered her clothes. "I should probably put these on before I go out in the hall, but I'd rather not."

"I dare you to streak back to your room."

She laughed. "It would probably be a very private streak. Judging from the way everyone looked at us last night when they found out about the necklace, they're convinced we spent the night together. They won't venture up here until they know we're both decent." She bundled her clothes together and decided streaking was the way to go.

He picked up his shirt from the floor. "Are you okay with everyone knowing?"

She glanced at him. "I'm okay with it. Are you?"

"Meg, I'm damned proud that you considered me worthy of being your lover. I don't care who knows it."

She smiled with relief. "That makes two of us, then. See you downstairs, cowboy." She opened the door, looked both ways and scurried back to her room.

Once she was there, she remembered leaving her necklace in his bathroom. Streaking once was one thing. Doing it twice was plain unnecessary because she was now in possession of the white terry bathrobe she'd packed.

Pulling it on, she tied the sash and started back down the hall just as Rafe walked out of his bedroom in all his naked glory. He spied her and paused, a smile spreading over his whiskered face.

She was mesmerized. At close quarters, while she'd been involved in either lovemaking or conversation with him, she hadn't been able to gauge the full impact of his athletic body. But when she had both daylight and perspective, she was struck by how magnificent he truly was. Michelangelo must have had someone like Rafe in mind when he sculpted David.

Well, except for the naughty bits. She'd always

thought David could have used a little more abundance in that department. Rafe outshone him there.

He chuckled. "So, are you planning to stand there all morning?"

"I will if you will. It's a great view."

"Flattery will get you everywhere, lady."

"I'm just telling the truth." She walked toward him. "That desert island is sounding better and better. You wouldn't ever have to get dressed as far as I'm concerned."

"No fair." Once she was within reach, he drew her into his arms and tugged at the belt of her robe. "I want my naked nurse back."

"I hear people bustling around downstairs." But when he opened her robe and pulled her close, she didn't object. She'd been admiring him from afar, and now she could enjoy the pleasure of feeling all those delicious lines and angles against her body.

"What people?" He leaned down and nuzzled behind her ear. "Aren't we the only two in the world?"

"'Fraid not." She cupped his firm buttocks and wanted him again. But the house was waking up, and although she didn't mind everyone knowing she'd spent the night with Rafe, she didn't want the family to think she couldn't tear herself away from him this morning.

"Too bad." He stroked her breast. "Your nipples are puckering up like they do when you want me."

"I *do* want you."

"Aha!"

"But I'm not going to act on it."

He continued to caress her. "So why did you come back?"

"For my necklace."

He chuckled. "What a great excuse." He started maneuvering her toward the bathroom. "Let's go get it, and while we're in there, we can—"

"Nope." She finally found the willpower to wriggle out of his arms and retie her robe. "You're quite tempting, Rafe Locke, but it's time for us to make an appearance."

He gave her a sad smile. "Can't blame a guy for trying."

"I'm thrilled that you're trying. Knowing you want me after all the sex we've had is…well, it's just very exciting."

"For me, too. I'm glad you still want me."

"I do." She took a deep breath. "And I would count it a huge favor if you'd go into the bathroom and bring out the necklace."

"Sure." He walked into the bathroom, giving her a tantalizing view of his tight buns in motion. Just inside the door he glanced over his shoulder. "Caught you looking."

"Why wouldn't I?"

"Good point. I'd do the same in your place." He continued into the bathroom and quickly returned holding her necklace. "So how about taking off your bathrobe before you walk back to your room? I wouldn't mind having that image to sustain me through the day."

She hesitated. She didn't *think* anyone would come upstairs unannounced, but she couldn't be positive.

"Come on, my uninhibited lover." He held out the necklace. "Need this for courage?"

"Maybe." She took it from his hand and settled it around her neck. The silver was cool against her hot skin, and she couldn't deny she felt different when she wore it.

A woman who wore a necklace this beautiful would have poise to spare. She'd accept the challenge of walking away naked from a man who wanted to admire her from behind. She'd revel in the power of her body to captivate him and hold him hostage to her whims.

"Take off the robe, Meg," he urged softly. "Take it off and walk away from me, knowing that I'll be devouring the sight of your bare ass every step of the way. I'll watch you go, and I'll want you desperately. If you turn to look before you go in, you'll see how much."

She lifted her chin and met his hot glance. "I'll do it."

"Is it on your list?"

"It is now." Untying her robe, she let it fall open and relished the way his eyes darkened in response. Slowly, keeping her gaze locked with his, she drew the robe off her shoulders and let it slide down.

Before it hit the floor, she grabbed the collar and held on. "See you downstairs, cowboy."

His throat moved as he swallowed. "You bet."

She took her time turning around, and then she strolled down the hall dragging the robe behind her as if it were a mink coat. She'd never been a runway model, but she'd seen the suggestive way they walked, and she was a good mimic.

Her heart thudded wildly as she put herself boldly on display for the man she'd loved so thoroughly the night before. She'd dared much with him, but always in the heat of passion. This deliberately provocative move was strictly solo, and it required a sexual confidence she hadn't thought she possessed.

At her doorway, she turned.

Rafe's soft laughter drifted toward her, and he gestured toward his rigid cock. "See?"

Gratifying indeed. "Hold that thought."

"Don't worry. I won't forget that visual for a long, long time. Now if you'll excuse me, I'm going to take a very cold shower."

"Sorry."

"Believe me, it was worth it. See you later, sweet cheeks."

"Which cheeks are you referring to?"

He laughed again. "I think you know." And then he was gone.

Moments later she heard the noise of the shower. Looping her robe over her arm, she walked into her bedroom. Strange, but she didn't feel like the same person who had left it yesterday.

15

DESPITE MISSING OUT ON another romp with Meg, Rafe was in a fantastic mood as he finished dressing in some of his new clothes. He liked the way they fit, and damned if he didn't feel a little more like a cowboy this morning.

Maybe cowboys had better sex. He wasn't opposed to making use of the fantasy this week, especially because it included having great sex with a woman he liked very much. He had several more days to be with her and find out if the magic continued. Assuming it did, he'd build more time into his schedule to be with her. And then…then they'd see.

He still had a thriving business in San Francisco and he wasn't about to let go of that. But if she was as captivated by their relationship as he was, she might be willing to make some concessions. After all, she was the one who'd already decided moving was an option.

Keeping that possibility under wraps seemed to be the best idea. No sense in stirring up opposition to the plan before he'd decided if it had value. He had one more unobstructed day with Meg. He hoped they could go riding. With that in mind, he tucked a condom in his jeans pocket. Never hurt to be prepared.

His cell phone lay on the dresser. He felt a little guilty for not paying more attention to his clients in the past couple of days. But hey, if any of them had lucked out and found a hot partner like he had, they'd do the same.

Maybe he should turn on the phone, though, and see how many messages had stacked up. He'd take a quick inventory and then go downstairs and have breakfast with Meg. Skipping breakfast had been a mistake yesterday, and he tried not to make the same mistake twice.

Fortunately, he didn't have a ton of work-related emails, but he had two missed calls from his father and finally the guy had decided to leave a message. He probably hadn't expected Rafe to turn off his phone because he so rarely did that. Rafe keyed in the message function.

Probably something about his dad's flight on Thursday. Maybe the landing time had changed by two minutes. Harlan Locke was a stickler for details, and his plane travel always turned into an elaborate schematic that probably drove his secretary around the bend.

Putting the phone to his ear, he prepared himself for an account of Harlan's exact ETA and his instructions for meeting at baggage claim. Rafe loved his anal father, but sometimes he had to shake his head at the minutia involved in Harlan's every move. Still, that attention to detail was probably one of the factors that had made his father a wealthy man.

Harlan's message had to do with his flight, but in a totally uncharacteristic move, he'd decided to change his schedule and come in a day early. Rafe was still adjusting to that news, which blew a hole in his plans with Meg for today and tonight, when his father dropped the bombshell.

"I'm switching my flight because your mother is coming to the wedding. She'll arrive on Friday, and I expect pandemonium when she gets there. I'd like an extra day to acquaint myself with Wyatt's bride before Diana blows everything apart."

Sinking to the edge of the bed, Rafe stared at his phone. So much for his happy little vision of spending the next few days getting to know Meg better. His father was arriving at noon today, and his mother would descend on them two days later. All hell was about to break loose.

He sent his dad a quick text promising to be at the airport at the appointed hour. Maybe he should ask Meg to come along. Nah, probably a bad idea.

Instinctively he knew that Meg and his father wouldn't get each other. She was full of optimism and enthusiasm for this event, while his dad planned to stoically endure the experience. Conversation might be strained on the ride home.

After pocketing his phone, he took a long, calming breath, put on his borrowed hat and left his room. Nothing had changed, really. He and Meg wouldn't have the same opportunities to be together, but after what they'd shared last night, she wouldn't give up on him because of that. They'd adjust.

He walked into the kitchen to find Meg sitting huddled at the table with Mary Lou and Sarah. Meg wasn't wearing her necklace, but that made sense if she thought they'd go riding later. The mood at the table was somber, though, and he had to believe they'd heard the news about Diana. All of them clutched their coffee mugs like life preservers.

Sarah glanced up the minute he walked in. "I don't know if you've heard, but Diana—"

"Is coming to the wedding. My dad left me a message. Has anyone told Wyatt?"

"Yes." Sarah met his gaze. "Diana did. She called Wyatt late last night, but he'd turned off his phone, so he didn't get the message until this morning. He called me a few minutes ago."

"But she won't be here until Friday," Rafe said, as if that made it more palatable.

"I don't know if that's good or bad." Sarah heaved a sigh. "She won't be here to cause problems with the advance preparations, but she'll show up when the festivities are in full swing. I won't have as much time to...to..." She spread her hands. "Come to think of it, I don't know what I'd do if I had more time. I guess we'll see what happens."

"She won't cause any problems," Mary Lou said. It sounded more like Mary Lou's personal threat than a considered opinion.

"I hope not." Rafe took off his hat, ran his fingers through his hair and repositioned the hat. "If it's any consolation, I'll do my best to keep her under control. I'm not saying I'll succeed, but I'll do my best."

Sarah nodded. "I appreciate that, Rafe. And just so you know, Wyatt seemed happy that she was coming. He's a sensitive guy, so he realized I might not be overjoyed, but...actually, I am glad. It's time."

Rafe thought about Wyatt, who of course wanted his mother to attend his wedding. The guy had a heart the size of Wyoming and hoped everyone would join hands and sing "Kumbaya" around a campfire. Then Rafe remembered the other player in this drama. He looked at Sarah. "Has Wyatt called Jack?"

She shook her head. "He hadn't when he contacted me, so I volunteered to do it. I called over to Jack's house, and Josie said he was on his way here to consult with Emmett about one of the new foals. I suppose he'll go straight to the barn."

"I'll go down there and tell him," Rafe said.

Sarah looked relieved. "Thank you. I think that's a good idea. He may have some questions I can't answer."

"There's one other thing. My dad is coming in today at noon instead of tomorrow." From the corner of his eye he saw Meg blink in surprise. "Now that my mother's arriving on Friday, my dad wants to meet Olivia before everything gets too…"

"That's fine." Sarah put down her mug. "I'll make sure his room's ready. Are you still picking him up, or is Wyatt?"

"I am." Initially he'd wanted to help ease his father's entry into country life by using the Lexus. Wyatt would have picked him up in his truck with the camper shell, or Olivia might have driven her Jeep. Neither one would have suited his dad. But maybe Rafe shouldn't be so concerned about whether his dad would feel comfortable with his transportation.

"I'll go with you," Meg said.

He hesitated. Not ten minutes ago he'd decided that wasn't a good idea.

"Unless you'd rather I didn't," Meg said.

In that instant he realized he wanted her there. If his dad had a problem with her sunny attitude, too bad.

Rafe's loyalties were shifting. "I'd love for you to go," he said. "I wasn't sure you'd want to."

"He'll be curious about Olivia. I'm her best friend, so I can tell him lots of great stories about her."

"Good. Let's leave about ten-thirty."

"I'll be ready."

Now that she was going with him, he was grateful she'd asked. The drive to Jackson would give them a chance to be alone before his father arrived. He wasn't thinking of it in sexual terms, because they'd need to keep close track of the time. But that drive might be their last opportunity to really talk.

"Rafe," Mary Lou said, "after you speak with Jack, I want you here in this kitchen for a decent breakfast. I'm not in favor of grabbing a cup of coffee and leaving, like you did yesterday. A body can't survive on that."

Rafe grinned at Meg. "You ratted on me, didn't you?"

"I might have said something." She did her best to look innocent and failed.

"That's fine." He discovered he rather liked having her look after his welfare. "I nearly starved to death yesterday after skipping breakfast. I promise to come back and eat whatever you put in front of me, Mary Lou."

She winked at him. "That's a deal, cowboy. And by the way, nice duds."

"Yes, they are," Sarah agreed. "Sorry I was so distracted that I didn't say anything. Meg, did you help him pick out those clothes?"

"Uh-huh." Her cheeks turned a becoming shade of pink.

He'd bet good money she was remembering the scene in the dressing room. And after all that, he hadn't modeled the leather vest for her last night. Now it was too late.

Or maybe not. Upstairs might not be their sanctuary anymore, but the ranch was a big place. He'd probably have to get creative, but it seemed a shame to waste the potential of that leather vest.

He touched the brim of his hat the way he'd seen other cowboys do. "Be back soon, ladies." He left the kitchen.

"Thanks, Rafe," Sarah called after him.

Walking quickly through the house and out the front door, he paused on the porch to take in the view of the Tetons. He still couldn't understand how his mother could have looked upon that view every day and yet failed to mention it as a feature of ranch life.

She must have been blinded by unhappiness. Rafe couldn't imagine being that unhappy, but then again, he wasn't convinced he knew his mother all that well. As he walked down to the barn, he tried to put himself in Jack's place. If he were Jack, how would he take this news?

Jack's outward behavior indicated that nothing would faze him. He projected strength and control. But Rafe knew through Wyatt that Jack wasn't as invincible as he seemed. His fear of abandonment, created by Diana, had taken years to overcome.

Rafe's allegiance was also shifting toward Jack, the man who had taught him to dance without making fun of him, the man who'd been willing to look like a fool while the two of them navigated through a Texas Two-Step. And yet, Diana was Rafe's mother. He couldn't turn his back on her, even if she deserved it.

What a mess she'd made for her three sons. Jack

might want to hold himself aloof from her, while Wyatt would be campaigning for a group hug. And Rafe... Rafe would be in the middle, trying to keep the drama from ruining what should be a perfectly good wedding and whatever chance he had at a relationship with Meg.

Jack's red truck was parked down by the barn. Judging from the advance billing he'd been given, Rafe would have expected Jack to drive a badass black truck. Instead he had picked out a truck that was, as he phrased it, *whorehouse-red.* Now that Rafe knew the guy a little better, he could see Jack gravitating toward a flashy truck.

Rafe wished he was headed down there to tease Jack about their dancing gig the night before instead of bringing the news about Diana. But he felt good about offering to do it. Sarah had enough to deal with.

She had been given the job of cleaning up the mess Diana had made more than thirty years ago. No telling what conflicting emotions were going through Sarah's mind right now. But she was one of the most gracious women Rafe had ever met, so he knew when the time came, she would act with dignity. He couldn't be so sure about his mother.

When he reached the open barn doors, he stopped to pet both dogs. The scent of horses, leather and hay stirred memories of his ride yesterday with Meg. Maybe if they came home from the airport early enough, they could take a quick ride before dinner. He wasn't sore, and he credited all the good sex for keeping his muscles warmed up most of the night.

Inside the barn he followed the sound of voices to a large stall where a mare and foal were stabled. Emmett and Jack leaned over the side of the stall watching mom and baby as they talked business.

Rafe couldn't help contrasting this business setting with his office back in San Francisco. He'd never expected to call the skyscraper where he worked cold and sterile, but in comparison to a barn full of beautiful horses, it was. He was a financial advisor, though, not a cowboy. He'd do well to remember how he earned a living.

Jack glanced up. "Hey, there, twinkle toes. I've never met a man who picked up the Texas Two-Step that fast. I'd say you cheated if I hadn't seen the way you stumbled through the Electric Slide when we first got started."

"Guess you're just an excellent teacher, Jack."

"Don't give me that. It was like a dance switch got flipped in your brain."

"Actually it was the karate switch."

Jack stared at him. "Come again?"

"I was into martial arts for quite a few years. At some point last night I called up the intense focus I once used for karate."

"Huh." Jack nodded. "That makes sense, then. You're like a Texas Two-Step ninja." He turned toward Emmett. "You should try dancing with this guy. He's good."

Emmett grinned. "No, thanks. But I'm sure sorry I missed the performance last night."

"Yeah, we were damned impressive." Jack looked over at Rafe. "Judging from your expression, you're a man on a mission. What's up?"

Rafe decided not to sugarcoat it. "Diana's coming to the wedding." He used her name instead of saying "my mother" or "our mother." He didn't know if Jack claimed her as his.

Shock registered for a split second in Jack's eyes before a mask of indifference obscured the emotion. "Okay."

"She called Wyatt this morning. She's flying in on Friday."

"Good to know." Jack's expression was unreadable. "Where's she staying?"

"She's… I don't know. I didn't think to ask."

"Your dad's staying here at the ranch, isn't he?"

"Yes, and that's the other thing. Dad's coming in today at noon instead of waiting until tomorrow. He's decided to get acquainted with Olivia before my…before Diana arrives."

"Smart man," Jack said.

Emmett stepped forward. "Look, it's none of my business, but I wonder if maybe we should ask Pam to put Diana up at the B and B. Pam runs a nice place, and it might be better all the way around."

"Depends on whether she has transportation," Jack said. "Do you know if she's planning to rent a car? Because I can tell you right now, I'm not hauling her ass around." He glanced away from Rafe and tugged on the brim of his hat. "Sorry. I keep forgetting she's your mother."

And yours. But Rafe had a feeling Jack didn't think of her that way and might never think of her that way. Sarah was his mother in every sense except biologically.

"I'll find out if she's planning to provide her own transportation." The Lexus would hold both of his parents, but Rafe didn't want to be the one chauffeuring them in the same car if he could possibly help it. "If she's not, maybe I'll suggest it, along with the B and B option. I've forgotten the name of the place. What's it called?"

"The Bunk and Grub," Emmett said.

"Perfect." Rafe imagined his mother's reaction to staying in a place named The Bunk and Grub. As Wyatt had said, their father was somewhat of a snob, but Diana took snobbery to a whole new level. The next few days would be a real circus. Unfortunately, he felt like the ringmaster trying to control the inevitable chaos.

16

To Meg's surprise, Rafe spent a good part of the drive to Jackson asking questions about her job. He wanted to know things she never expected anybody but another engineer to care about, and he seemed interested as she described the traffic flow challenges when cities like Pittsburgh grew in unexpected ways.

As they talked, she wondered if Rafe was focusing on traffic in Pittsburgh because it beat thinking about his parents' imminent arrival in Jackson Hole. If he needed a distraction, she was happy to provide it. And it was fun for her. Most men she'd dated had avoided mentioning her work.

Rafe didn't bring up his parents until they stood side by side in baggage claim waiting for Harlan Locke to deplane. "Wyatt takes after my dad," he said. "Dad has some gray mixed in with his sandy hair, but his eyes are the exact same gray as Wyatt's. Temperamentally, though, they're nothing alike."

She glanced over at him. "I don't know if you remember saying the same thing about you and Wyatt the day we met."

"Did I?"

"You did, but personally I think you and your brother are more alike than different."

"It's the outfit making you say that. Underneath this Western shirt beats the heart of a big-city guy who loves to wheel and deal in the market. Wyatt hates that kind of thing. He'd rather climb a mountain."

"But you both crave a challenge, even if they're different challenges. I'll stick to my opinion."

He smiled. "You do that. But when it comes to my dad and Wyatt, they really are different. He— Never mind. Here he comes. You can see for yourself."

Harlan Locke strode toward them looking like a Ralph Lauren model, trim and sophisticated in an open-throated white silk shirt and tan slacks that—defying the logic of plane travel—remained crisp. He'd slung a leather computer case over one shoulder and he held a cell phone to his ear. Lifting a hand in greeting, he continued to talk to whoever was on the phone as he walked in their direction.

Meg told herself the phone call might be important, and Harlan had seen his son recently. It wasn't as if they'd been apart for months. But surely Harlan had noticed that Rafe had brought a friend. She thought he should get off the phone soon and greet those who had come to fetch him.

She hung back a little, though, wanting to give father and son a moment together before Rafe introduced her. The man continued to talk on the damned phone while Rafe stared at the floor and waited for his father to finish the call. Meg fumed on Rafe's behalf.

He'd been telling the truth when he'd said his father and Wyatt were completely different. Wyatt would never have put a phone call, any phone call, ahead of greeting someone who'd come to meet him. She had to believe Rafe wouldn't, either.

Finally Rafe turned and beckoned her to come over. Might as well. She wouldn't be interrupting a warm moment between father and son.

More time passed in which Harlan glanced at them, rolled his eyes, but kept talking. Finally he took the phone from his ear and disconnected the call. "Sorry about that. A client's favorite stock just tanked and I had to talk him off the ledge. I tried to warn him to pull out weeks ago, but he wanted to hang on."

Rafe put a hand against the small of Meg's back. "Dad, I'd like you to meet the maid of honor, Meg Seymour."

"Delighted to meet you, Meg." Harlan held out his hand.

Meg shook his hand and smiled. "I'm glad to meet you, too, Mr. Locke." She was glad, if only to understand Rafe better.

"Call me Harlan, please. *Mr. Locke* makes me feel old."

"Harlan it is, then." She guessed that age was a sensitive topic with him. With twenty-nine-year-old sons, he had to be in his fifties, yet he could pass for someone ten years younger.

"I see your bag," Rafe said. "I'll go grab it."

"Thanks." Harlan turned back to Meg. "Nice of you to come along and keep Rafe company on the airport run."

"I wanted to. Olivia and I have been best friends for most of our lives, so I'm the advance promo team for her. You're very lucky to get her as a daughter-in-law."

"That's what Wyatt tells me. I'm hoping she will convince him to get serious about this trekking business of his."

"Oh? I thought he was already quite committed to it."

Harlan shook his head. "To the work itself, I suppose, but he's blind to the growth potential. He never should have closed his San Francisco operation and moved everything here. He could have put someone else in charge up there and made this a second location. I've been advocating expansion for years, maybe franchise the concept. Colorado, Arizona, Florida, maybe even go international with it."

"I don't know. It's hard to imagine Wyatt as a tycoon."

Harlan laughed. "Isn't it, though? Rafe, on the other hand, is well on his way to making his first million. I wish Wyatt had some of Rafe's business sense."

"Got your suitcase." Rafe appeared pulling a Gucci rolling bag that probably cost the same as two months' rent on Meg's condo in Pittsburgh.

She hadn't thought to investigate what sort of suitcase Rafe had brought. Probably one like this if he could so easily recognize his father's. And he had bought her a necklace with a gasp-worthy price tag.

According to his dad, Rafe was on his way to making his first million. That was intimidating. She'd tried to push Rafe's sophisticated lifestyle to the back of her mind because it pointed up their differences. Maybe she'd be wise to remember those differences did exist.

Harlan murmured his approval of the Lexus when they loaded his suitcase in the trunk. Meg urged him to sit up front with Rafe, but he insisted on taking the backseat. As he climbed in, his phone chimed.

For most of the ride back to the Last Chance, Harlan took calls on his cell phone. Meg tried making conversation with Rafe, but she felt weird talking over Harlan so she finally gave up and rode in silence.

"He's on the phone a lot," Rafe said in a low, apologetic voice.

"So I see. Business must be good."

"Oh, it's very good. I used to think he worked hard to provide luxuries for my mother, but now that they're divorced, I realize he just likes working hard."

"Mmm." Meg had a million thoughts running through her head and couldn't voice any of them. Someone had once told her that if you wanted to see what a man would be like in twenty-five years, look at his father. Meg shuddered to think Rafe would turn out like this.

As they neared the outskirts of Shoshone, Harlan ended a call and, amazingly, his phone didn't ring right away. "So, Rafe, looks like you've gone native. Never thought I'd see you duded up like a cowboy."

"It's more practical to dress like this. Turns out I like to ride."

"Horses?"

"Yeah, it's the damnedest thing. Meg taught me the basics, and we went out on a trail ride yesterday. I enjoyed the hell out of it."

"Will wonders never cease. Just don't try to get me on one of those animals. I like my transportation to have a steering wheel and foot pedals. So this is Shoshone, huh?"

"This is it."

"Not much to the place, is there?"

Meg turned toward the backseat. "Depends on how

you look at it. For anyone who prefers the simple life, then it's perfect."

Harlan laughed. "Yeah, Wyatt's told me all about the *simple* life around here. He warned me not to expect decent espresso or full-service day spas in Shoshone. He mentioned one bar, one diner, an ice cream shop, a gas station and a feed store. Did I miss anything?"

"That about covers it," Rafe said.

"I don't know how you've been surviving, Rafe. You must be going stir-crazy."

"Actually, I haven't." Rafe glanced over at Meg and gave her a secret smile. "It's been a nice break from my usual routine."

"I doubt if I'll be able to say the same on Sunday, but I can't let my son get married without showing up and meeting the bride. I'll tell you this, though, I can see why Diana left. A wide spot in the road wouldn't suit her at all."

Rafe stopped the Lexus at the town's only traffic signal. "So, Dad, what about her parents? Did she ever tell you about them?"

"Only that her mother was a full-blooded Shoshone and her father was Anglo. Apparently they died."

"At the same time?" The light changed and Rafe pulled through the intersection.

"I think so, yeah."

"Was there a traffic accident, or what?"

"I don't know, Rafe. You'll have to ask her." His tone indicated that the subject was closed as far as he was concerned.

"It just feels strange to think that they were my grandparents, but I know nothing about them."

"Does it matter?" Harlan sounded slightly irritated.

"They won't be any good to you at this point. You had Nana and Papa Locke while you were growing up."

Meg wished she could lay a comforting hand on Rafe's arm, but she didn't want to telegraph anything about their relationship to Harlan. Rafe was asking perfectly legitimate questions, things she'd want to know in his shoes, but his father displayed no empathy at all. What a shame.

Harlan's phone chimed soon after that, and he returned to his business.

"There might be a way to research your grandparents," Meg said softly. "Do you know your mother's maiden name?"

"Not off the top of my head. But it would be on my birth certificate back in San Francisco."

"What about Wyatt's birth certificate?"

He sent her a look of gratitude. "You're a genius." He took out his cell phone and hit a button. "Hey, bro. Yeah, we have the parental unit in the car. Listen, can you put your hands on your birth certificate? I want to know Mom's maiden name."

He paused to listen. "Well, I thought I'd research our grandparents and find out…You did already? How come you didn't tell me?" His expression slowly changed from excitement to sadness. "Yeah, I can see why you wouldn't be eager to share that in the middle of happy times. But it's good to know. Yeah, thanks. See you tonight." He disconnected the phone and sighed.

"What did he say?"

"He had the same questions I did, so a couple of weeks ago Olivia helped him track down the information. He didn't tell me then because it's not all that positive, and Wyatt likes to dwell on the positive."

That made her smile because it was so true. "Will you tell me anyway?"

He glanced at her and then checked the rearview mirror. His father was still on the phone. Rafe lowered his voice. "Wyatt found somebody who actually knew them. They were heavy drinkers, and they chain-smoked, too. My mother had gone to a teenage slumber party the night her parents got drunk, as usual. They accidentally set fire to the house and they both died in the fire."

Meg gasped softly. "Oh, Rafe." She squeezed his arm, no longer caring if Harlan noticed.

"You can see why Wyatt wasn't ready to lay that on me in the middle of all the wedding festivities. I wonder if Jack knows. I have to believe he doesn't or he wouldn't be so hard on my mom. Something like that… well, it helps explain a few things."

"I'm sure." Meg had been prepared to dislike Diana even more than she already disliked Harlan, but knowing this sad tale changed her knee-jerk reaction. She'd been willing to condemn a woman who would abandon her child. But in a way, Diana had been abandoned, too.

When they reached the ranch, Sarah must have been watching for them, because she came out on the porch to greet Harlan as warmly as she might have welcomed an old friend. Fortunately Harlan didn't walk up the porch steps while talking on his cell phone. He was all charm and courtesy as they went into the house.

That irritated Meg even more. If Harlan saved his disrespect only for his nearest and dearest—and, by extension, their friends—that would be worse than if he treated everyone in the same high-handed way. It was as if his status as father and former chief breadwinner gave him the right to ignore common courtesy with his own children.

He might very well have shown the same arrogance with his wife, now his ex-wife. Once again, Meg decided she needed to reserve judgment until she'd met Diana and could get a sense of the woman. But the jury was in on Harlan Locke. She didn't like him.

"So, what do you think of my dad?"

She'd been so lost in thought that Harlan and Sarah's departure hadn't registered. She and Rafe stood alone in the living room. And he'd just asked her a question she didn't want to answer.

"It's okay, Meg," he said gently. "I didn't think you'd get along with him."

"We haven't had much time to talk." *Because he's been on the phone.*

He chuckled. "Let me rephrase that. You're from completely different planets."

She sighed in relief at being given a graceful way out of the discussion. "Yes, we are." And his father was from the Planet of the A-holes, but she wasn't going to say that out loud.

"It's funny, but I used to accept that he'd be on the phone all the time whenever I was with him, but this afternoon I saw it through your eyes. It's kind of obnoxious, isn't it?"

"Let's say I wouldn't do that."

"And I hope to hell that *I* wouldn't do that, but they say the apple doesn't fall far from the tree. I'm going to pay more attention to my phone habits from now on."

"You haven't been the least bit obnoxious with your phone since I've known you."

He trailed his finger down her cheek. "That's probably because you're such a good influence on me."

"Darn it! And here I hoped that I was a bad influence, the kind of wild woman who parades down hallways naked."

Heat flared in his dark eyes. "I'll never forget that. And just so you know, I'm not giving up on having some alone time with you. We'll go make out in the barn if we have to, but I—" He paused and glanced toward the staircase as Sarah and his father started back down. "Later."

She winked at him. "You bet, cowboy." Her heart felt considerably lighter knowing that he could accept her reservations regarding his father.

"I just talked to Wyatt," Harlan said as he made his way back over to where Meg and Rafe stood. "He'd like to meet up in about thirty minutes at that bar we passed on the way in—the Spit and Spots, or something like that. He's bringing Olivia."

"It's the Spirits and Spurs." Sarah's voice had lost some of its welcoming warmth. "My daughter-in-law Josie owns it."

"Oh. Sorry. I didn't get a good look at the sign when we drove through." Harlan turned back to Rafe. "So I said we could probably do that."

"We can." Rafe glanced at Meg. "Would you like to come along?"

"Thanks, but I really need to do a few things around here." She was moving from mild dislike to active dislike when it came to Harlan Locke, so the invitation held little appeal for her. Besides, she wanted Livy to form her own opinion without picking up negative vibes from her best friend. They could compare notes later.

Rafe looked as if he'd hoped for a different answer, but he gave her an understanding smile. "Right. I'll see you at dinner, then."

"Yes, I'll see you then. Nice to have met you, Mr. L—uh, I mean Harlan."

"Same here, Meg."

With one last glance in Meg's direction, Rafe followed his dad out the door.

Sarah let out a deep sigh. "And he's supposed to be the good parent."

Meg nodded. "And speaking of Diana, I just heard something you might want to know before she arrives."

"Let's go get a cup of coffee and sit out on the porch while you tell me about it." Then she smiled. "Archie and Nelsie sometimes added a little Baileys to their coffee when they felt the need. I'm feeling the need. How about you?"

"Absolutely, Sarah." Meg was so glad she'd stayed home instead of riding into town. "Hook me up."

17

As the hours went by, Rafe asked himself if his father had always been such an arrogant snob and had to admit that he had. Rafe had excused his behavior because the guy worked so damned hard, but his dad seemed to believe that dedication to his work made him superior to everyone else.

That sense of superiority hadn't been so obvious in Harlan's own environment when he was surrounded by people like him. But here it stood out in stark relief. Seeing his father as the Chances surely did was disorienting.

He'd looked up to his father all his life and considered him a role model. He'd followed in his dad's footsteps, partly because he had a natural ability when it came to money management, but partly to please his dad. Harlan *was* pleased, and made sure to tell everyone at the dinner table that night how financially successful Rafe had become under his tutelage.

With every self-congratulating word out of his father's mouth, Meg's attitude grew more distant. Rafe could see it in her eyes. She didn't much like his father, and the more Harlan referred to Rafe as a "chip off the old block," the less she was going to like Rafe. He needed to reconnect with her.

As everyone left the dining table to gather in front of the fire in the living room, Rafe drew Meg aside. "Could I interest you in a walk in the moonlight, little lady?"

Her answering smile was tentative. "Wouldn't it be rude to do that when the evening's still in progress?"

"Not if I come up with an excuse. Leave it to me."

She still looked doubtful. "All right."

As everyone sought chairs and Sarah offered after-dinner drinks, Rafe spoke up. "I could be wrong, but I think there's a partial eclipse tonight. Meg and I are going out to take a look."

"An eclipse?" Wyatt frowned. "I don't remember hearing about that."

"That's because you're obsessed with wedding plans," Jack said. "I heard about it." He looked over at his wife. "Didn't you, Josie?"

"No, I—oh, wait, yes, now that you mention it." She ducked her head and suddenly became very busy playing with little Archie.

Rafe felt a surge of gratitude toward Jack and Josie. They knew he'd made up the eclipse story and were helping substantiate it.

"I heard about it, too," Olivia said. "You two go check it out for the rest of us."

"We'll do that. Come on, Meg." He hustled her outside before any more questions were asked.

"An eclipse?"

"There could be." He took her hand as they went down the steps to the gravel driveway. "You never

know. Let's go see." He led her into the shadows created by two giant blue spruce trees on the far side of
the drive.

She laughed. "Don't you need to be out in the open
to look at the moon?"

"That's one theory." He pulled her into his arms.
"We can discuss it later." Then he kissed her with the
desperation of a man who'd gone too long without feeling her lips on his.

She kissed him back, but her response felt subtly different. Instinctively he knew she wasn't giving herself
to the experience the way she had before. She'd injected
a note of caution into her kiss.

Reluctantly he lifted his head. "Talk to me, Meg."

"What do you want to talk about?"

He couldn't see her expression very well in the shadows, but he didn't have to. He heard the hesitation in
her voice. "Tonight at the dinner table I felt you pulling
away. Was I wrong?"

"Rafe…"

Icicles settled in his gut. "I know my dad's been getting on your nerves, but I'm not him. I hope never to
be like him."

With a sigh, she cupped his face in both hands.
"I'm sure you won't, but listening to him I realized
how truly different you and I are. You're focused on
making money, and I'm focused on being happy. That
makes our goals and values miles apart."

"What if making money makes me happy? I enjoy
my work, Meg. How much I earn doing it is a way of
keeping score. Is that so terrible?"

"No, it's not terrible at all. It's just different from
my way of looking at things. We have different pri-

orities. I've been kidding myself that we could extend this…whatever is going on between us…longer than this week, but—"

"We can." He drew her closer. "I refuse to believe we're as far apart as you say. I love my job and you love yours. And by the way, I can't see your job transferring to Jackson Hole, but I'm sure you could find something in San Francisco. You'd love the challenges of that city, Meg. There's heavy traffic, hills and trolley cars. You could really sink your teeth into the problems there."

She grew very still in his arms. "Is that why you were asking me about my work today? So you could convince me to give up Jackson Hole and put San Francisco in its place?"

"Not exactly. I was curious about how you planned to make that transition, and I really can't see it happening easily here. But in a city the size of—"

"I don't want to move to another big city, Rafe. Living here would make me happy."

"Will you be happy if you're unemployed? Not doing the work you love? I don't think so."

"You know what? I'm not worried about how the job situation will work out. If I can't get hired in my field, I'll find something similar. I have some savings, and I can live on that until I figure out my next step. But if I can hang out in this area, ride horses, admire the mountains and learn to ski, then I'm going to do whatever it takes to make that happen."

"Wow." He took a deep breath and gazed up into the branches of the spruce towering above them. "You're more of a free spirit than I thought."

"Then you weren't listening," she said gently. She

stroked her hands from his cheeks to his shoulders. "Rafe, what we've had was great, but I think it's time to—"

"Don't say that."

"I have to say that. I was starting to fall for you, but after tonight I realize how crazy that is. I—I'll return the necklace."

"The hell you will."

"It's far too expensive a gift for a woman you spent only one night with. I don't care how well-off you are, that's a ridiculous extravagance."

His heart broke slowly and painfully into dozens of pieces. "Look, it's been a long day, and neither of us got much sleep last night. We shouldn't be having such a heavy-duty discussion right now."

Giving his shoulders a squeeze, she stepped out of his arms. "Rafe, I care for you, but I also care for myself. I'm not going to continue toying with an emotional connection that has the power to derail my plans to live a happy life. I refuse to allow you to make me miserable."

"So you don't care if you make me miserable?"

"Of course I do. But my first obligation is to myself. I know who I am and what I want out of life. It's not the same as what you want." She took a shaky breath. "I'm going in."

"Sure. Okay. I'm going…down to check on the horses." He had no idea if the horses needed checking or not. He didn't know if that was the sort of thing that cowboys did on a ranch. But the barn felt like a refuge right now, and he needed one.

Fortunately the place wasn't locked up. All he had to do was lift the bar across the double doors, and he was in. No overhead lights were on, but soft lights placed at ankle-height along the aisle between the stalls kept him from stumbling around in the dark.

So he was here in the barn, with its comforting scents of hay, horses, leather and old wood. Now what? He wandered down to Destiny's stall. Although he'd hoped for at least one more ride with Meg, that probably wouldn't happen.

Destiny looked up expectantly as Rafe leaned against the stall door. Belatedly he realized that paying a visit like this might work out better if he'd brought some carrots or apples. "I got nothin', Destiny," he said. "Sorry."

The horse came over anyway, and nudged Rafe's arm. Rafe stroked the white blaze that ran from Destiny's forehead to his wide nostrils. "She doesn't want me, horse. Simple as that. I guess she's looking for some guy who doesn't give a damn where his next paycheck is coming from."

Destiny snorted and pawed the straw with one hoof.

"I know. That's nuts, but what can I do? I'm not going to give up a client list worth seven figures so I can hang out with her in some tiny house in Shoshone." But as he said it, the pieces of his broken heart throbbed. It didn't sound so bad.

"But sure as the world, we'd be *poor,* Destiny. There's nothing noble about being happy and poor. I don't care what she says. I—" He fell silent as the sound of booted feet came down the aisle between the stalls.

"Kinda hard to see an eclipse if you're in the barn," Jack said.

"Turns out I was mistaken about the eclipse."

"I know." Jack walked over and leaned against Destiny's stall, facing Rafe. He had on his hat, which made

Rafe wish he'd worn his tonight, but he hadn't felt right doing it. Chalk one up for his dad's influence.

"I was just trying to help you out by going along with that eclipse nonsense," Jack said. "But when Meg came in alone, I figured everything had gone south."

"So you came down here to check on me?" That made Rafe feel somewhat better.

"Hell, no. I came down to check on the horses. I like doing that. There's a peaceful feeling about a barn full of horses at night."

Rafe let that stand, but he still had the impression Jack was here on account of him, not the horses. "As long as you're here, let me say one thing. My dad's a pain in the ass. I won't apologize for him because it's not my responsibility that he acts like that, but I will acknowledge it."

"The good part is, he's proud of you."

"I wish he'd keep that to himself. His bragging didn't help the situation with Meg. But then, that was probably doomed, anyway."

"How so?"

"We look at things completely differently."

"Then it's good you found that out now, before either of you got in too deep."

"Right." Rafe nodded. "Right." Maybe eventually he'd convince himself of that. But he ached for her so much that he couldn't believe the pain would ever go away.

"Incidentally, on a totally different subject, Sarah told me the story about how our grandparents died."

Rafe gazed at him. "Not pretty."

"No. I talked to Wyatt for a little while. He figured

out that Diana was seventeen when that happened. Do you remember what you were doing at seventeen?"

"Chasing girls and driving over the speed limit, mostly."

"Me, too." Jack grimaced. "Stupid stuff. I had a home and people who cared about me, not that I appreciated it. She had none of that. I guess she was in foster care for a little while, but mostly she was on her own."

"Jack, I still don't think that excuses what she did."

"It doesn't. But I see her differently now." He glanced up. "You ready to go back up to the house and grab us a couple of brewskies?"

"As long as it doesn't involve dancing."

"Nope. I'm saving myself for the party tomorrow night. If I get enough beer in me, I might ask Harlan to dance."

Rafe laughed. "I'd pay to see that."

"Yeah? How much? Lay some money on the line, and I'll be even more motivated."

"Let's just say I'll make it well worth your while."

"That's good enough for me." He clapped Rafe on the shoulder. "Word on the street is that you're loaded."

"Don't believe everything you hear."

"Okay, but if you're even half as rich as your dad says, you need to invest in a sure thing. I have this awesome stallion named Houdini, and a person could do very well with a percentage of his future stud fees."

"You're probably kidding, but I kind of like the idea."

"I am kidding. You don't want to do that. Breeding horses is a fool's game, but my brothers and I love it. The only way we'll ever get rich is by selling the ranch, and we have no intention of doing that."

Rafe remembered his first thoughts when he'd arrived here. "Do you have a good financial advisor?"

"We do, but he's getting old, about to retire. Are you volunteering for the job?"

Rafe thought about it as they closed up the barn and walked back to the house. "Yeah, I am. But let's use the barter system. I'll take over as your financial planner in exchange for room and board whenever I come to visit my brother."

"Deal." Jack stuck out his hand. "I assume you know Meg's planning to relocate here."

"So she said."

Jack nodded. "Thought so. Just checking."

Rafe told himself that his offer to be the Last Chance's financial planner had nothing to do with Meg. But in his heart he knew it had everything to do with her. In spite of their differences, he didn't want to lose touch with her, so if he kept in contact with the ranch, he'd always have a link to Meg Seymour.

THE THRILL HAD GONE OUT of the wedding plans so far as Meg was concerned. She went through the motions and tried to inject some enthusiasm into the activities for Olivia and Wyatt's sake. But every time she caught a glimpse of Rafe, she wanted to cry.

She'd told him that she wouldn't allow him to make her miserable, but…she was miserable all the same. The bachelor/bachelorette party was especially painful because she'd had such high hopes of dancing the night away with Rafe. Instead he danced with everyone else, including Jack.

At one point Jack tried manfully to get Harlan out on the floor, but it didn't work out. Meg wasn't surprised. Rafe's father didn't have a spontaneous bone in his body.

Rafe, however, threw himself into the party with gusto. No groom could ask for a more spirited best man than Rafe. As requests poured in for a repeat of Rafe and Jack performing the Texas Two-Step, they finally surrendered to the inevitable and danced together amid catcalls and wild applause.

Meg applauded as loudly as anyone. In spite of everything, she loved seeing Rafe moving out of his comfort zone and attempting things that might make him look foolish. Once he was back in San Francisco, that could all change, but at least he was able to step up for Wyatt's wedding.

After Rafe's dance with Jack, Meg lost track of him until he appeared unexpectedly at her side.

"I think it's customary for the best man to have a dance with the maid of honor," he said.

Her heart beat in triple time as she glanced up. He looked wonderful in the clothes she'd helped him choose in Jackson. He'd worn his borrowed hat tonight, and he blended in so well that an outsider wouldn't have been able to tell he wasn't one of the local cowboys.

"I think it's customary at the wedding reception," she said. "But a bachelor/bachelorette party isn't in the manual."

"So is that a no?" His voice was low, but there was a trace of raw disappointment there.

"Actually, it's a yes." Grabbing his hand, she drew him onto the floor. "But I'm probably not as good a dancer as Jack."

He swung her into his arms. "No, but you probably won't keep trying to lead the way he does."

"No, I won't." His touch made her slightly dizzy. She hadn't realized how much she'd missed him until she twirled in his warm arms and surrendered her hand to his firm grip.

He executed a turn with smooth efficiency. "Wyatt and I took a ride today."

"I heard that." She'd tried not to feel bereft that he'd gone riding without her. "How'd it go?"

"Great. That's something we'll enjoy doing together when I visit, and I have you to thank."

"I'm glad it's worked out."

"Damn it, Meg, I miss you."

She looked into his eyes. "I miss you, too."

"We had something special going on. I can't believe that it—"

"Great sex doesn't equal a good relationship, Rafe."

"It's a damned good start. Come down to my room tonight. We can talk."

She smiled, although her refusal was killing her. "We wouldn't just talk and you know it. I thought I could have sex with you and let it go at that, but I can't. I want more, and that's foolish. We're headed in different directions, you and I."

"But this is torture."

"Hang on until Sunday. Then it'll all be over." She didn't believe that for a minute. She'd be months getting over Rafe, and maybe longer. But at least once the wedding had passed, she wouldn't have the agony of seeing him every day.

18

TEN MINUTES BEFORE THE rehearsal was scheduled to begin in the ranch house living room on Friday afternoon, Diana hadn't arrived. Rafe didn't even know if she was in town yet. Her phone had been turned off for hours.

He paced the hallway between the living room and the dining area because windows all along one side gave him a view of the front driveway. He could also have waited on the porch, but he'd be damned if she'd find him standing out there waiting the way he had so many times as a kid.

When he'd sent her a message yesterday suggesting that she stay at the Bunk and Grub and rent a car at the airport, she'd replied *Fine*. That was the last he'd heard from her. Maybe the suggestions had pissed her off and she'd decided to stay home, after all.

Rafe had mixed emotions about that. Personally he'd be relieved, but Wyatt would be upset. Jack would be royally ticked off after he'd mentally prepared himself for this meeting. So would Sarah, and anyone else who'd been around thirty-plus years ago, like Emmett and Mary Lou.

So on balance, Rafe wanted to see a rental car with his mother at the wheel pull up in front of the ranch house within the next ten minutes. He glanced at his watch. Correction, nine minutes.

"Any sign of her?" Meg came down the hallway from the direction of the living room. Like everyone else today, she'd dressed casually in jeans and a T-shirt.

"No sign of her, but this is typical. She creates drama wherever she goes, so I'm not surprised."

"It must be hard on you, though." She stopped a short distance away. She'd been maintaining that physical distance recently, even though her expression and her tone of voice told him she was worried about how he was handling the stress.

He'd manage a hell of a lot better if she'd let him hold her. But he wasn't going to beg. Even so, he looked forward to the rehearsal because she'd be forced to take his arm during the recessional.

He missed touching her more than he'd expected to. His body yearned for hers with a fierceness that kept him from sleeping at night and caused him to seek her out during the day. All morning he'd had a good excuse to hang around her because the whole family had pitched in to decorate the living room for tomorrow's ceremony.

Rafe knew Wyatt and Olivia were thrilled with the results. The ranch hands had carted the heavy living room furniture out to the tractor barn, where it would stay until tomorrow night. In its place all thirty-two dining chairs had been arranged in rows. They would provide plenty of seating because the guest list was small.

Tyler Keller, Alex's wife, had supervised the decorating, which included piling flowers in the empty fireplace and draping vines all over the stones to create a backdrop for the minister and the wedding party. White satin bows adorned each chair, and more flowers in vases gave the room a chapel-like atmosphere.

He glanced toward the driveway again and sighed. "It's not as hard on me as it is on Wyatt. I've accepted what she's like, but I don't think he ever has. He keeps hoping she'll be different."

"I've tried putting myself in her shoes," Meg said. "How would it feel to walk into a place where no one is happy to see you?"

"Nobody, that is, except Wyatt. He'll be glad."

"Okay, one person, then. But a bunch of others who've condemned you for your past actions." She met Rafe's gaze. "If she comes, I give her props for it. She may have done some things that weren't cool, but if she shows up, it proves she has guts."

"I suppose it does. But you're not going to like her, Meg. If you think my father's obnoxious, wait until you've met my mother."

She regarded him quietly for a moment. "Please know that it's not because of your parents that I've decided we don't belong together."

"Oh, so it's just me, then?" He tried to make a joke out of it even though she was slicing him to ribbons. "Gee, I'd rather blame it on them, if you don't mind."

"No, it's not you, either! You're fine. Wonderful. We're just not in sync!"

"Funny, but I remember a few times we were perfectly in sync. I don't know if you realize this, but simultaneous orgasms aren't the most common thing in the world, and yet we—"

"Don't, Rafe." A flush spread over her cheeks. "You'll only make it harder."

"Now who's talking dirty?"

"Make it more *difficult!* Sheesh!"

She was adorable. And he, poor sap, was in love with her. He couldn't convince himself that she was in love with him, though.

Sure, she cared about him or she wouldn't be here helping him sweat out this waiting game. But if she loved him, she'd want to find a way they could be together. Instead she was ripping them apart.

Yet, like a fool, he looked into her green eyes searching for something, anything that would give him hope. As he did, he could swear that her expression relaxed a little, and a soft glow warmed her eyes. Or maybe he was imagining things. Before he could be sure, she turned toward the window.

"Rafe, somebody's coming."

He looked, and sure enough, a little Jeep had turned into the gravel drive. Although it was the kind that could lose its top and side doors for off-roading, it was buttoned up tight.

"Is it her?"

"I can't believe she'd rent a Jeep, but that's my mother getting out." And she was wearing…holy crap. She was wearing jeans. And boots. True, they were red, but they were cowboy boots, not designer heels.

Her sequined red T-shirt was more her style and she had on her trademark Gucci shades. Her hair had recently been colored and styled and hung straight and shining to her shoulders. She looked terrific, but he couldn't get over the jeans and boots. He'd never seen her wear anything remotely Western.

"Are you going out to meet her?" Meg asked. "I think that would be a nice gesture, all things considered, so she doesn't have to walk in cold."

"You're right." Without thinking, he grabbed her hand. "Come with me."

She seemed startled, but she didn't jerk away from him. "I don't know if that's a good idea."

"I do. Besides Wyatt, you may be the only person who's giving her the benefit of the doubt."

"Okay, then." She hurried with him down the hall.

"She's here!" Rafe called as they passed through the living room. "Meg and I will go get her."

"We'll go, too," Wyatt said. "Come on, Olivia."

The four of them piled out of the door and started down the steps as Diana rounded the Jeep clutching several shopping bags in each hand. Now that was a familiar sight. His mother was one hell of a shopper.

She paused uncertainly when she saw them. "Wow, a welcoming party."

"You bet, Mom." Wyatt walked forward with Olivia. "This is Olivia Sedgewick."

"Hello, Olivia. I'm so glad to meet you." Diana's voice trembled slightly. "You're beautiful." She turned to Wyatt. "She's lovely, Wyatt. Just lovely." And then, to everyone's total surprise, tears started running down from under her sunglasses and onto her cheeks. "I'm sorry." Still holding the bags, she reached one hand to wipe her face, knocked off her sunglasses and slammed the bags into Wyatt's chest. "Oh, dear. I'm m-making a mess of this."

Rafe squeezed Meg's hand and let go. "Let me take

those bags, Mom." He was seriously rattled. He'd never seen his mother cry.

"Oh, thanks." She sniffed and handed them over. "It's…it's presents…f-for Wyatt and Olivia. I didn't know what they needed, so I put g-gift receipts…"

Wyatt folded her in his arms. "I'm sure we'll love all of it, Mom."

Rafe grabbed up her sunglasses from the gravel and stood holding the bags, unable to take it all in. His mother was crying. And wearing jeans and boots.

"Let me hold those," Meg said softly. "You go to your mother." She pried the bags and sunglasses out of his hands.

In a daze, he walked over and put his arms around his mother and Wyatt as she continued to cry and apologize in alternating waves. Rafe couldn't decide if she was apologizing for crying, for being late, or for a million and one sins that she'd been accumulating her entire life.

But this wasn't the mother he'd thought he knew. For the first time in his relationship with her, his throat hurt from joy instead of disappointment. She did love her sons, after all. Until this moment, he'd never been really sure.

"Okay, okay," Diana said. "Enough. Back up, you big lugs, and let me get hold of myself." Eyes still streaming, she waved her carefully manicured hands in front of her face. "There goes the Elizabeth Arden makeover."

Rafe laughed with a certain measure of relief. That sounded more like the old Diana. Except as he gazed at her puffy eyes and red nose, he realized something else. "I love you, Mom," he said quietly.

"Me, too." Wyatt squeezed her shoulder. "Thanks for coming to my wedding."

"I wouldn't have missed it for the world. I—" She caught her breath as she glanced at the porch and her hand covered her heart. Silently her lips formed a name. *Jack.*

Rafe turned as Jack came slowly down the steps, his gaze never leaving Diana. Rafe and Wyatt both stepped aside but Rafe was prepared to move in if necessary. He wouldn't abandon his mother now.

She trembled as Jack came nearer, his dark eyes, so like hers, unreadable.

He stopped when he was within arm's length of her. "I wanted to hate you." His voice was strained. "You left a little boy who didn't understand why you'd disappeared."

"I know," she whispered. "Jack, I…" She gulped and blinked very fast.

"I understand a little better now. I'm not excusing you for what you did."

"No." Her voice was thick with emotion. "Nothing could excuse it."

"But I…" He held out both hands. "I don't want to live with anger anymore."

She grabbed hold of his hands and hung on. "I will always live with regret."

"Yeah, me, too." He squeezed her hands. "But it's time to move on." He glanced at Rafe and Wyatt. "Having a couple of bonus brothers isn't so bad, and I hear that one of them is trying to get himself married."

"Right." Diana gave a quick nod, as if willing herself back under control. "I've held things up long enough." She sniffed hard and gazed up at the sky. "Damn, it's blue up there. I'd forgotten how blue the Wyoming sky is."

Then she looked over at Meg. "In all the confusion, I don't think I met you." Walking forward, she held out her hand. "I'm Diana Locke."

"I'm Meg Seymour, the maid of honor." Meg grasped Diana's hand in both of hers. "I'm happy to meet you."

Rafe smiled as he remembered his discussion with Meg that only one person would be happy to meet Diana. After this display of vulnerability on his mother's part, he hoped there would be more. The fact that she'd dressed like a cowgirl and driven up in a Jeep would help.

Diana glanced over at Rafe. "If I'm not mistaken, you came down the steps holding this delightful young woman's hand. Does that mean you're…friends?"

Rafe's heart hammered as he looked at Meg. "Yes, we're friends." But that wasn't all of it, and this didn't seem to be a day for half truths. "No, that's not exactly right. I'm in love with her, Mom."

Meg gasped.

"I see." Diana gazed at Meg. "And how about you? Are you in love with my son?"

Meg gulped. "I… Yes, I'm afraid so."

Rafe's jaw dropped and he stared at her. "You are?"

"But, Rafe," Diana said. "Notice how she phrased it. She said she was 'afraid so,' which means she's in love with you but doesn't think that's wise. Why isn't it wise, my dear?"

Meg took a deep breath. "Because Rafe is focused on the bottom line, and I'm focused on living a happy life, regardless of the bottom line."

"Did he tell you that?"

"Pretty much."

Rafe's mother waved a dismissive hand. "Don't believe a word of it. That's his father talking. Rafe has the most loving heart in the world and he'll never be like his father, no matter how hard he tries."

"And I'll second that opinion," Wyatt said. "Besides, I've seen the way he looks at you, Meg. If you want the guy, you've got him. You just need to tell him how high to jump."

"Hey!" Rafe glared at his brother. "What kind of talk is that?"

Wyatt laughed. "I know what I know, bro. And now I'm going to do you a big favor and get this whole crowd inside so you and Meg can have a little one-on-one. But don't get carried away. We have a rehearsal coming up."

Rafe stood there thinking about what Wyatt had said as Olivia took the shopping bags from Meg and everyone walked inside. He'd been thinking that if Meg loved him, she'd find a way for them to be together. What about the fact that he loved her? Shouldn't he be finding a way?

Well, he had. He'd suggested she move to San Francisco, but city life wouldn't make her happy. He used to think city life made him happy, but how happy would he be without Meg?

Besides, he'd become mighty fond of this ranch and this area. He imagined himself living here, and got excited about the idea. But he couldn't live here and keep his client base in San Francisco…or could he? Why not? So much of his communication was via the phone and the internet. He could always fly back to the city every now and then to have face-to-face meetings.

"You're not saying anything." Meg continued to stand several feet away.

He looked at her with renewed focus, and everything

fell into its logical place. Of course she was the one. And he was the one for her. "That's because I'm waiting for you to tell me how high to jump."

"I doubt you'd be willing to jump that high, no matter what your mother and Wyatt think."

He smiled, because he was so many steps ahead of her. "Try me."

"I personally think you could live in Shoshone and telecommute with your clients, but I doubt that you—"

"I would." He enjoyed the shock that widened her eyes. "In fact, I'd need to try and keep as many of my San Francisco clients as possible because it looks like I'll be earning the lion's share of the family income. You're not going to have an easy time finding a job around here."

"I know, which is why I've come up with a different plan." Her eyes narrowed. "Wait a minute. Did you just refer to a 'family income'? What family are you talking about?"

"Ours." He crossed the distance between them and took her by the shoulders. "Because, Meg Seymour, we're going to marry each other and have kids who will grow up learning to ride, and rope, and ski."

"Is that a proposal?"

"It is, but you're worrying me with this alternate plan of yours. I want us to live here, so I hope you're not about to throw a monkey wrench into that plan."

"You're *proposing?* It doesn't feel like a proposal."

"Why not?"

"For starters, you're not down on one knee."

"You have a proposal scenario on your list, right?"

"Yep."

"Alrighty, then." He dropped to one knee and spread

out his arms. "Done." Then he patted his knee. "Sit here."

"That's not part of the scenario on my list."

"Then it should be. Come here." He smiled at her. "Please."

"Oh, okay." She balanced on his knee and wrapped her arms around his neck. "You were saying?"

He cleared his throat. "Meg Seymour, will you do me the honor of becoming my wife?"

"This is rather sudden."

"I know." He gazed into her eyes. "But tell me honestly, aren't you crazy about me?"

She laughed. "Yes, you egomaniac, I am."

"And I'm crazy about you. And it's not the sort of deluded crazy that gets people into trouble. We fit and we both know we do, once we figure out the whole career/living arrangement thing. So is that figured out or not?"

"It is. I'm going to start a consulting business helping cities experiencing unexpected urban growth and I'll base it here. I'll have to travel, which means you might become the babysitter. Are you okay with that?"

"I'll be happy to babysit our kids if you'll marry me. I know some couples have kids without getting married, but I'm sort of old-fashioned about that, so I'd want the ring, the license, the ceremony, the whole deal."

"Then I guess I'll have to marry you."

"Good. Now that we've settled that, I'm going to kiss you. I didn't want to do it while we were still negotiating, for fear you'd accuse me of taking unfair advantage."

"Oh, please do. That sounds like fun."

"It will be. I promise." He kissed her as thoroughly

as he dared while balancing her on one knee. Falling into the gravel would not be cool.

But, glory and hallelujah, she kissed him back with all of her heart and soul. He'd experienced her kiss when she was holding something back, but that wasn't the situation now. She was giving him everything she had to give.

And he was giving everything he had, too. For the first time in his life, he was laying himself bare because love demanded nothing less. As he reluctantly ended the kiss and they walked hand-in-hand back to the house, he thought about the event that had led to this moment. More than thirty years ago, his mother had made a choice that changed everything. Although some condemned her for that choice, he would be forever grateful.

Epilogue

NASH BLEDSOE WAS LATE to the wedding. No one would notice, because he hadn't planned to be there, despite a personal invitation from his good buddy Jack Chance. Nash's life was a mess, and although he wished the best for Jack's half brother Wyatt and Wyatt's bride, Olivia, he hadn't seen his way clear to attend their nuptials.

Last night, however, he'd thought of all the reasons why he *should* be there. He'd thrown a few things in the car, left his bachelor pad in Sacramento, and headed for the Last Chance Ranch.

As he drove in this afternoon, he took note of the outdoor wedding reception area that had been set up with a platform for dancing, tents in case of rain, and gaily decorated tables and chairs. If it was like most Chance events, it would be a blowout. After parking his truck in an area to the left of the circular drive, he mounted the familiar front porch steps.

Damn, he'd been away too long from a place that he'd cherished from the time he was a little kid. Maybe coming here would help him sort through his options. Ending his marriage to Lindsay had been necessary, but now he had to figure out what the hell he wanted to do with his life.

The ceremony was in progress. As he quietly opened the front door, the minister repeated the words that Nash remembered hearing three years ago when he'd thought Lindsay was his forever-after soul mate. He hoped those words would work out better for Wyatt and Olivia than they had for him and Lindsay.

Slipping inside, he quickly saw that all the chairs lined up in the living room were filled. Jack had said it would be a small wedding, about thirty people, and Nash had felt honored to be included, even if he'd had to send his regrets. Fortunately no one noticed him come in. He would have hated to interrupt the ceremony.

He searched the crowd and found his mother, Lucy, still a redhead thanks to regular salon visits. Sure enough, she was sitting next to Ronald Hutchinson, a widower who ran the local feed store. That was one of Nash's reasons for coming today. His sister Katrina had mentioned that Lucy and Ronald had a romance going on, and Nash felt he should check that out in person.

Katrina hadn't been able to get home for the wedding, though. She trained thoroughbreds back East, and work had kept her away. Just as well, considering Nash's other concern, the guy seated on his mother's far side. Langford "Hutch" Hutchinson, Ronald's son and a talented sports videographer, had been Nash's friend since they were kids.

In fact, Hutch, Jack and Nash had been close all through school and into their twenties before life had gotten in the way. But Hutch was severely testing that friendship. Nash was still trying to sort out the particulars, but he gathered from what Katrina was *not* saying that Hutch had seduced her this past spring when they both happened to be in town. Furthermore, he hadn't proposed marriage afterward.

Katrina might be fine with that, but Nash wasn't. In his estimation, any guy who messed with his sister had better show up the very next day with a ring and a plan. Katrina had made no mention of a ring, and the plan seemed to be continuing with their careers on opposite sides of the country.

Nash's dad had died seven years ago, which made Nash the man of the family, the one assigned to watch out for the womenfolk. The Hutchinsons, both father and son, had been fooling around with the Bledsoe women. Nash was here to find out their intentions.

Although that had been his primary goal in driving over, he admitted to being curious about Jack's two half brothers, Wyatt and Rafe, who'd turned up out of the blue. Rafe was handling the best man duties, and if Nash squinted slightly, he'd swear it could be Jack standing up there. The striking resemblance confirmed that Rafe and Jack were half brothers. Wyatt's body build was similar to Jack's, but his coloring was much lighter, so he must take after his dad.

Jack had also said there was a slim possibility that Diana, mother to Jack, Wyatt and Rafe, might show up for the wedding. Nash was pretty sure he'd spotted her because she had features that reminded him of Jack. After witnessing firsthand the damage she'd done, Nash wasn't inclined to be friendly.

He decided to take his cue from Jack on that one. If Jack had made peace with the mother who'd abandoned him more than thirty years ago, then Nash would do his best to suspend judgment. But he'd witnessed Jack battling his demons as a result of Diana's actions, and Nash figured Diana had plenty to answer for.

Nash recognized most of the other wedding guests, who were either members of the Chance family or close friends. But he puzzled over the identity of an old codger in the front row. The guy could pass for Albert Einstein—same wild hair and a nutty professor outfit consisting of a tweed sports coat and plaid pants. Because he sat up front, Nash guessed he was related to Olivia.

The minister finished, and Wyatt was invited to kiss Olivia. Cheers erupted from the guests, who gave the couple a standing ovation. Nash stepped aside to let the happy couple fly past him and out the front door, followed by Rafe and a woman he didn't recognize.

Next came the one most likely to be Diana, escorted by a guy in an expensive-looking suit. He was dry-eyed, but she was in tears. Nash didn't have much time to think about her, though, because the next person down the aisle was Sarah. Nash, along with everyone in town, considered Sarah Jack's real mother.

"Nash!" She stepped out of the procession and rushed over to give him a hug. "You made it!"

"Better late than never." He hugged her back and wished he'd accepted the invitation right off the bat. So what if his life was in the dumper? His old friends wouldn't care about that.

"This is Pete Beckett, my fiancé. I can't remember if you've met him."

"I don't think so." Nash shook the guy's hand. "But congratulations. You're getting a gem."

"I know." The light in Pete's eyes when he looked at Sarah convinced Nash he really did know he'd lucked out.

Nash hoped the same could be said for the Hutchinsons, both father and son. After promising Sarah a dance at the reception, he looked around for his mother. She'd spied him. Bypassing the central aisle, she'd come around the chairs from the other direction and was bearing down on him, trailed by the Hutchinson duo.

"Nash Bledsoe, did you drive straight through? You did, didn't you? You know I hate when you do that." Then she gave him a fierce hug. "Glad you got here safely, you big lunk-head."

"Me, too, Mom." He hugged her back, but over the top of her head he found himself eye-to-eye with Ronald Hutchinson, and behind Ronald stood Hutch, looking decidedly uneasy. As well he should.

Nash called up his most intimidating stare, the one he'd used to great effect against opposing linemen back in high school. "So, Mom, what's this I hear about the Hutchinson men making off with the Bledsoe women?"

His mother laughed as she stepped back and smiled up at him. "Crazy, isn't it? First Ronald was courting me, and then your sister came to town, and…the rest is history, as they say."

Nash's gaze flicked to Hutch, who was trying to look innocent. Ha.

Ronald came forward and offered his hand. "For the record, I plan to spoil your mother rotten."

"Glad to hear it." As Nash shook the guy's hand, he relaxed on his mother's account. Ronald seemed as smitten with Lucy as Pete Beckett was with Sarah. But that still left the issue of Katrina and Hutch.

"Well…" Lucy glanced from Nash to Hutch as if feeling the tension between them. "We'll get on out to the reception. You boys haven't seen each other for a while. I'm sure you want some private time to talk."

"Yeah. See you out there later." Nash was finally face-to-face with Hutch, and the years faded away. Suddenly they were teenagers again, and he felt the way he had when he'd caught Hutch ogling his sister in a bikini. Before he could censor himself, he swung.

His fist connected with Hutch's jaw and Hutch landed on his butt. He looked dazed for a moment, and then he rubbed his jaw and grinned. "Feel better?"

"Infinitely." Nash chuckled and shook his head, a little embarrassed at his gut reaction. "Sorry, buddy, but I had to get that out of my system. It's the big brother thing."

"I do understand. Would it help if I said I'd spoil her rotten? That seemed to work for my dad."

"Yeah, but I believe your dad." Nash extended his hand and pulled Hutch to his feet. "You, my friend, are going to have to prove it. So, are you buying her a big old rock or not?"

Hutch's grin widened. "As a matter of fact, I am, but she doesn't know that yet, so I'd appreciate it if you wouldn't go blabbing to her."

"Excellent!" Nash clapped him on the shoulder. "If you're putting a ring on her finger, then my work here is done."

"You're not leaving, are you?"

"No, at least not until I've congratulated the bride and groom. But I have a messy divorce to clean up back home, and—"

"Are you planning on staying in Sacramento, then?"

Nash had debated that for weeks. "I don't know. We're selling the stable, so…"

"Jack would give you a job in a second."

"I know, but I hate to trade on friendship for a job."

"Bullshit. You're a good hand and he knows it. You've always loved this place. Why not move back for a while, see how it goes?"

"I might. You know, I just might." The idea sounded better the more he considered it. "Right now, though, we have a wedding reception going on outside. And if I remember right, the Chances know how to party."

"They certainly do," Hutch said. "Good booze, good music, pretty women. What more could you want?"

"At the moment, not a damned thing. Let's go." But as Nash headed out to the wedding reception with his friend, he knew that in the long run he wanted more, much more. Maybe, just maybe, he could find it at the Last Chance Ranch.

* * * * *

COMING NEXT MONTH from Harlequin® Blaze™
AVAILABLE AUGUST 21, 2012

#705 NORTHERN RENEGADE
Alaskan Heat
Jennifer LaBrecque
Former Gunnery Sergeant Liam Reinhardt thinks he's fought his last battle when he rolls into the small town of Good Riddance, Alaska, on the back of his motorcycle. Then he meets Tansy Wellington....

#706 JUST ONE NIGHT
The Wrong Bed
Nancy Warren
Realtor Hailey Fleming is surprised to find a sexy stranger fast asleep in the house she's just listed. Rob Klassen is floored—his house *isn't* for sale—and convincing Hailey of that *and* his good intentions might keep them up all night!

#707 THE MIGHTY QUINNS: KIERAN
The Mighty Quinns
Kate Hoffmann
When Kieran Quinn comes to the rescue of a beautiful blonde, all he expects is a thank-you. But runaway country star Maddie West is on a quest to find herself. And Kieran, with his sexy good looks and killer smile, is the perfect traveling companion.

#708 FULL SURRENDER
Uniformly Hot!
Joanne Rock
Photographer Stephanie Rosen really needs to get her mojo back. And who better for the job than the guy who rocked her world five years ago, navy lieutenant Daniel Murphy?

#709 UNDONE BY MOONLIGHT
Flirting with Justice
Wendy Etherington
As Calla Tucker uncovers the truth about her detective friend Devin Antonio's suspension, more secrets are revealed, including their long, secret attraction for each other....

#710 WATCH ME
Stepping Up
Lisa Renee Jones
A "curse" has hit TV's hottest reality dance show and security chief Sam Kellar is trying to keep control. What he can't control, though, is his desire for Meagan Tippan, the show's creator!

You can find more information on upcoming Harlequin®
titles, free excerpts and more at www.Harlequin.com.

HBCNM0812

REQUEST YOUR FREE BOOKS!
2 FREE NOVELS PLUS 2 FREE GIFTS!

◆ Harlequin®

Blaze

red-hot reads!

YES! Please send me 2 FREE Harlequin® Blaze™ novels and my 2 FREE gifts (gifts are worth about $10). After receiving them, if I don't wish to receive any more books, I can return the shipping statement marked "cancel." If I don't cancel, I will receive 6 brand-new novels every month and be billed just $4.49 per book in the U.S. or $4.96 per book in Canada. That's a saving of at least 14% off the cover price. It's quite a bargain. Shipping and handling is just 50¢ per book in the U.S. and 75¢ per book in Canada.* I understand that accepting the 2 free books and gifts places me under no obligation to buy anything. I can always return a shipment and cancel at any time. Even if I never buy another book, the two free books and gifts are mine to keep forever.

151/351 HDN FEQE

Name _____ (PLEASE PRINT)

Address _____ Apt. #

City _____ State/Prov. _____ Zip/Postal Code

Signature (if under 18, a parent or guardian must sign)

Mail to the **Reader Service**:
IN U.S.A.: P.O. Box 1867, Buffalo, NY 14240-1867
IN CANADA: P.O. Box 609, Fort Erie, Ontario L2A 5X3

Not valid for current subscribers to Harlequin Blaze books.

Want to try two free books from another line?
Call 1-800-873-8635 or visit www.ReaderService.com.

* Terms and prices subject to change without notice. Prices do not include applicable taxes. Sales tax applicable in N.Y. Canadian residents will be charged applicable taxes. Offer not valid in Quebec. This offer is limited to one order per household. All orders subject to credit approval. Credit or debit balances in a customer's account(s) may be offset by any other outstanding balance owed by or to the customer. Please allow 4 to 6 weeks for delivery. Offer available while quantities last.

Your Privacy—The Reader Service is committed to protecting your privacy. Our Privacy Policy is available online at www.ReaderService.com or upon request from the Reader Service.

We make a portion of our mailing list available to reputable third parties that offer products we believe may interest you. If you prefer that we not exchange your name with third parties, or if you wish to clarify or modify your communication preferences, please visit us at www.ReaderService.com/consumerchoice or write to us at Reader Service Preference Service, P.O. Box 9062, Buffalo, NY 14269. Include your complete name and address.

HB11B

Enjoy this sneak peek of USA TODAY *bestselling author*
Maureen Child's newest title
UP CLOSE AND PERSONAL

Available September 2012 from Harlequin® Desire!

"**L**aura, I know you're in there!"

Ronan Connolly pounded on the bright blue front door, then paused to listen. Not a sound from inside the house, though he knew too well that Laura was in there. Hell, he could practically *feel* her standing just on the other side of the damned door.

He glanced at her car parked alongside the house, then glared again at the still-closed front door.

"You won't convince me you're not at home. Your car is parked in the street, Laura."

Her voice came then, muffled but clear. "It's a driveway in America, Ronan. You're not in Ireland, remember?"

"More's the pity." He scrubbed one hand across his face and rolled his eyes in frustration. If they were in Ireland right now, he'd have half the village of Dunley on his side and he'd bloody well get her to open the door.

"I heard that," she said.

Grinding his teeth together, he counted to ten. Then did it a second time. "Whatever the hell you want to call it, Laura, your car is *here* and so are you. Why not open the door and we can talk this out. Together. In private."

"I've got nothing to say to you."

He laughed shortly. That would be a first indeed, he told himself. A more opinionated woman he had never met. He had to admit, he had enjoyed verbally sparring with her. He admired a quick mind and a sharp tongue. He'd admired her even more once he'd gotten her into his bed.

He glanced down at the dozen red roses he held clutched in his right hand and called himself a damned fool for thinking this woman would be swayed by pretty flowers and a smooth speech. Hell, she hadn't even *seen* the flowers yet. At this rate, she never would.

Huffing out an impatient breath, he lowered his voice. "You know why I'm here. Let's get it done and have it over then."

There was a moment's pause, as if she were thinking about what he'd said. Then she spoke up again. "You can't have him."

"What?"

"You heard me."

Ronan narrowed his gaze fiercely on the door as if he could see through the panel to the woman beyond. "Aye, I heard you. Though, I don't believe it. I've come for what's mine, Laura, and I'm not leaving until I have it."

Will Ronan get what he's come for?

Find out in Maureen Child's new title
UP CLOSE AND PERSONAL

Available September 2012 from Harlequin® Desire!